Kit and the Beeman

A Fantasy story for all ages

Geoffrey Foster

May 2008

Geoffrey Foster was born in London, England in 1933, and his childhood was mostly spent in the County of Kent, in southeast England. Some of the action of this book, which has occasional echoes of his own experiences, takes place in or around that area, which was semi-rural even when he lived there, and was certainly rural in the Middle Ages, the time of the book.

His father was a policeman most of his working life, and his mother, when she worked, was a shorthand typist (a stenographer). He has two sisters, five and thirteen years younger than himself.

He went to public elementary and secondary school and then to the University of Cambridge, where he studied engineering. Moving to Australia in 1959, he taught Mechanical Engineering at the University of Queensland for 14 years, before switching to educational development, running workshops and other activities for academics. Eventually he took early retirement in 1995.

As well as writing, he likes reading, listening to music, solving cryptic crosswords, walking the family beagle, Kafka, and playing a game with his younger sister, Ynes, that they whimsically refer to as 'tennis.'

Also by Geoffrey Foster and uniform with this volume:

Kit the Venturer

Vincent the Beeman

ISBN 978-0-9805310-0-8

Chapter One

On a thirsty summer's afternoon a young man was making his way across the downlands that swept north from the chalk cliffs of the coast. Although his clothes and boots were covered with the white dust that rose from the road, anyone could see from his dress and bearing that he was not a simple wanderer, but a person of some position and means. He was tall, lean and muscular, his face tanned, and his sun-bleached hair cut short of shoulder-length and tied back in a black ribbon. He wore no hat, there was a knapsack slung over his shoulder, and his long boots did not look meant for walking. At his side he wore, not the straight sword usually preferred by gentlemen of the times, but a curved cutlass in a rather battered scabbard of what might have been Eastern design.

His expression was distant, and his pace steady, for he was walking not only to cover the miles but to clear his thoughts. As he strode along he was only half aware of the road and the shimmering fields of gorse and heather to each side; his mind was filled with visions of his lost wife and children, and of the terrible wave that had taken them from him — was it really only two days ago?

Why had he let himself be persuaded to take them on board for a voyage abroad, however short? Why had he not kept them with him on deck that night, instead of putting them to sleep in his own bunk in his captain's cabin? Why had he not dived again and again, even till he drowned, instead of using his last strength to drag himself to shore without them? What would he say to his lost crewmen's families when he reached his home in the port city?

Through his silent litany of despair and guilt, he became aware of something small, moving behind him, only half seen from the corner of his eye. He forgot his torment for a moment and turned to see what it could be, but as he did he lost sight of it completely; he shook his head and returned to his sad thoughts.

A few minutes later he glimpsed it again, and this time was more careful as he turned; there it was, a bee or some other insect, like the many that buzzed and fluttered over the honey-laden heather and the yellow gorse flowers. But this one seemed to be

1

following him, keeping a few feet to one side and just behind him. As he quickened his pace and resumed his steady progress, it drew closer and more abreast of him.

Again he shook his head; he was not ready to leave his fretting yet. But the interruption had made him more conscious of his bodily feelings and of the surroundings. He realised that he must have been on the road for over six hours, and was footsore, as well as hungry and thirsty; he had taken nothing but a drink from a stream since he set off early, after a none-too comfortable night spent under some bushes.

Just off the track he saw a smooth rounded boulder set in a patch of green grass amid the heather; he sat down on this natural bench, wincing a little as the weight came off his back. He had walked farther this last day and a half than he usually did in a month. Off came his pack, and he bit eagerly into a green apple that he took from it, slaking his thirst a little before starting on a half-loaf of rye bread and a heel of cheese. He remembered with gratitude the cottager who had pressed him to accept them the previous day, after a good meal of soup and bread for which she had refused any payment.

Then he saw that his tiny companion had decided to rest too; it had settled on a tall thistle, only an arms-length from his seat. He peered at it, and saw to his amazement that it was not an insect, but a miniature winged horse. As he excitedly strained to see it, he could make out the perfectly made saddle and bridle, fashioned of what looked like the finest soft red leather. The stirrup-leathers were looped over the saddle, and the reins lay on the horse's neck. But of a rider, there was no other sign.

He sat up straight, his heart thumping, his head spinning and his sad loss forgotten for a while; was this a trick of fatigue, a delusion, or was it real? And if it was real, what was its story and its purpose? How had this fairy steed come to choose him as travelling-companion? Did it bring a message, or was this simply a chance encounter? There was no doubt there was magic here, but was it white or black?

As this thought came to him, he fumbled with his neckerchief and found the silver cross that had hung around his neck since his lost bride gave it to him on their wedding night; he was no church-goer, but he needed to grasp at something for reassurance. He held it fast and spoke aloud for the first time in two days, "If you be evil, then begone, I will have nothing to do with you!"

As he spoke, his voice cracked with the emotion of the moment, and his head swam, so that he almost missed hearing the faintest whinny as the horse tossed his head and flew from the thistle to his knee, landing there with hardly a touch. He shrank away from it a little, but made no attempt to brush it away. And then, this magic beast spoke to him in his own tongue, but so quietly that he had to muster up an intense concentration to hear what it said.

"Although I must seem a strange creature to you, Captain Stephen, I bear no malice to you or any human; I have come to you to be your friend, if you will allow me. I am the servant of one who knows of your honesty and good sense, one who wishes to console you in your grief, and even to restore the meaning to your life."

The traveller was dumbstruck, but after a few moments recovered his composure sufficiently to ask a flood of questions: "What are you, fairy or angel? Who is your master? How do you know my name? What will you do with me? How must I act?"

The horse whinnied again, shook its black head so that the silver fittings on its harness tinkled, and said in the same faint voice, "All these questions and more I will either answer myself or tell you who can, but for now you must be patient, for we have to act, not talk. Will you trust me, however strange you may think are the things I ask you to do?"

"Yes, oh yes," answered the man, in a fever of fearful hope, "how could I refuse, who thought to have nothing of value left in this life. Ask of me what you will; only tell me again that you do not cruelly deceive me, for I would rather die than be disappointed."

"I will show you a token of my trustworthiness," replied the horse, "put your hand into your knapsack."

Trembling, the young man opened his pack, and took out the contents: a cloak, a linen shirt, a razor and a hairbrush, and a pouch that he knew held but two or three silver coins. There, at the bottom of the knapsack, was something further: a packet wrapped in a linen cloth, that he had never seen before.

3

Opening it with fingers made clumsy by his apprehension he found that it was a picture, an exquisite painting in a leather frame, of a young gentlewoman, standing with her arms around the shoulders of a boy and a little girl. "My own loved ones," he cried, and fell to the ground in a deep faint.

Chapter Two

Stephen came to his senses to find the horse standing over him, shading him from the sun. What further magic was this? — the horse was now full-sized!

More, it was a noble steed, fit for any lord, or even the king of the country to ride upon. Now he did not need to squint to see details, he could marvel at the fine quality of the saddle and harness, the silken saddle cloth, embroidered with rich figures, and the fine grooming, bearing and hauteur of the horse.

"Get up on my back, sir" said the steed, and it was no longer necessary to strain to hear him. Quickly the young man threw his knapsack over his shoulder, slipped his foot into the stirrup and swung himself easily into the saddle. Oh how good it was to be mounted once more, how right it felt!

The saddle was as comfortable as though it had been made to his order; the stirrup leathers and reins were exactly as he liked to have them, and he knew that this wonderful horse was capable of doing anything he asked, almost as soon as he thought it.

Without waiting for a signal, the horse set off, walking at first, then trotting, following the road in the same direction as before. In the space of a few hundred yards it broke into an easy canter that the young man felt that it could have kept up for hours. Within a few miles the country began to look different and the gorse and heather gave way to a loose, low, woodland, with a few great oaks and beeches here and there. They came to at least two cross-roads, but went straight ahead at each. The road was descending now, and the horizon was no longer visible as a pale evening haze arose; the rider shivered, hoping that the temperature would not drop too much more, for he had only a thin cloak with him.

A pheasant started up noisily from bushes next the road, and this reminded the young man of something that had been puzzling him:

"Tell me, O horse, if it be a proper question, where are your wings, now that you have grown to full size?"

The horse turned his head toward its rider and said, in a friendly tone, "You may ask me anything, my lord, and I will answer as best I can. The answer to your question has two parts to it: first, we have no need of wings now, since we have only a few miles to travel and the road is fair. Second, we shall soon encounter men with whom we have business, and I do not wish to astonish them more than I have to; besides, there are those who are so frightened of magic that they might do me harm before thinking."

"Some further questions, then; where are we headed, who shall we meet, and what will be our business?"

The horse snorted gently, as though chuckling, and replied, still cheerfully, "Please, my lord, not too many questions at once! Perhaps it would be best if we took time to rest before we reach our destination; before too long, while we are standing or sitting still, I will tell you all you want and need. The light is failing and I must not stumble."

Indeed, the young man saw, the dusk was almost with them and the trees were crowding in, so that now they had to twist and turn around them, although it was evident, by felled trees and drifts of gravel in the muddy hollows, that some upkeep had been attempted on the road. Now they came to a fork, with one branch continuing the way they had been following, and the other smaller and seemingly less used. The horse chose the lesser, and after a few yards drew up.

"Please dismount, Captain," said the horse, "we shall rest near to here a while and take stock."

When the man had dropped to his feet, his steed led him through the bushes and saplings bordering the track; these grew so closely that both the travellers had sometimes to duck their heads or push aside boughs to make their way. After a short distance, no more than twenty yards, they came out into a small glade where there was an old hut or cottage, somewhat tumble-down and covered with moss.

The young man stretched and looked about him; it took him a moment to notice two significant matters: there was a thin ribbon of blue smoke rising from a hole in the roof of the hut and, coming from inside, the faint sound of someone singing a tuneless song, as though to accompany some sort of housework.

6

The horse tossed his head and nudged him in the shoulder, but without speaking, and he realised that it wished him to go into the hut. Slowly and uncertainly, he walked to the rough plank door, which stood slightly ajar, and rapped on it with his knuckles.

The singing stopped.

Chapter Three

The door was pulled open from within, and there in the doorway stood a stout man with a weathered red face fringed with grizzled hair and a week-old beard; he was dressed in clothes that might once have been worn by someone elegant but were now shabby and stained. His expression was a mixture of timidity and curiosity as he greeted his visitor: "Welcome, your lordship; will you take a glass and a bite with me in my poor lodging? My name is Rollo, and I am the King's road mender."

The young man was taken by such unquestioning hospitality, replying: "Why thank you, kind fellow; but I am no lord. I am but a captain without a ship, and they call me Stephen the Venturer. But first, where can my horse slake his thirst, for we have ridden far this afternoon?"

"Why, sir, there is a stream hard by the back of my house; let me lead your mount there. There is plenty of grazing hereabouts." Rollo took the bridle and led the horse behind the cottage, with Stephen following a step behind. When the horse saw the stream he lowered his head and drank deeply.

"Does he need tethering, my lord … Captain Stephen, sir?"

"No, no, give him his head so he may graze where he will," replied Stephen, and the two men returned to the front of the cottage, where there was a rough bench made from logs and a plank.

"Please take your ease, sir, as you can, and I will fetch you something to eat and drink; it will be humble fare, but if you are as hungry and thirsty as your mount, I doubt you will mind that."

After a few minutes, Rollo came out again, bearing a trencher with bread and country sausage, and two mugs of ale, saying, "May I join you, sir? I am ready for a meal myself."

Stephen motioned him to sit beside him, and both men set to with a will. When they had finished, the road mender said nothing, but looked inquiringly at his guest, silently inviting him to tell his story if he would.

"I told you I have no ship;" Stephen began, "I had a fine one until two days ago when she was wrecked but half a mile off the coast not far from here; but I still cannot understand how. The wind was fair and the tide running well when all of a sudden a great wave arose and fell on the vessel so that she filled and sank like a stone. I was cast into the water, but I saw no-one else; ten men, my wife, my son, my daughter, all are lost."

Stephen lowered his head and, at last, allowed the walled-up sobs and tears to come, while Rollo put his arm round his shoulders and held him, rocking him gently, as a father would comfort a hurt child.

A little later, as the light slowly faded, the two men sat and stared into a fire of twigs that Rollo had made to keep the evening chill at bay, and began to confide in each other, telling of their lives and of their situations with no desire to hold anything back, for each had felt drawn to the other, without quite knowing why.

Rollo told how he had been since he was a boy in the service of the lord of the manor in those parts; and how, more than ten years ago, his lord had refused to raise troops for the King, wishing to save his people from warfare. For this disloyalty he had been exiled, and his castle, lands and serfs seized by the King.

"But this was merciful," said Rollo, "for King Arnold had the right to put him to the gallows for such disobedience. Aye, the King is a good and just man, and I am proud to be his servant in more tasks than one."

"You told me that you were the King's road-mender, what other services do you give him?" asked Stephen. Rollo did not answer at once, and Stephen felt that he had perhaps been too pressing with his inquiry. But after pondering for a few moments, the older man seemed to make a decision, and, pouring his guest another mug of ale, leant closer so that his ruddy face was made even ruddier by the glow of the fire, and spoke.

"I suppose you could call me a sort of game-keeper of men, or you might say a spy if you were less kind. I keep watch on all the travellers that pass by here, and I tell the King's sergeant how many they be, what they claim their business is, and what I think of them. Although you might not think it, the main road lies close to this cottage, yonder, with only a line of trees between; no walker or rider who keeps to the road can slip by without me hearing and seeing him. The sergeant rides by every morning, and we sit and take some breakfast together while I make him my report."

"And what will you tell him of me, my friend? Do you judge that I am someone he should be wary of? Or will you give me a favourable bill of health?"

"Oh, sir", said Rollo, with a grunt of amusement, "if I had had any doubts about you, I would never have told you of my trade! I have lived long enough to know who to trust, who to test further, and who to avoid as I would a wolf or a tusky boar. The King knows this well, and that is why he relies on me, in these uncertain times."

Just then, as though in demonstration of Rollo's duties, the soft sounds of a horse's hooves on turf were heard. Rollo rose to his feet, with a spring surprising in a man who was no longer young, and turned toward the sound, ready to step through the bushes and see who it might be. But then he laughed once more, as Stephen's horse came into the firelight, "It is a friend, my lord; I shall not try to question him this time!"

The horse approached Stephen, bent his head close to his ear, and spoke quietly. Stephen at once glanced toward Rollo, to see how he would take this unusual behaviour, but his steed explained, "Do not be concerned, my lord, no-one but you can overhear my speech; he simply hears my quiet sounds as a murmuring whinny. What I must tell you is that we both need to take rest, for we have much to do in the morrow. If it please you, pay your respects to our host and ask where you may sleep. I can take my rest quite well where I stand, but if you could kindly take off my tack and trappings, it will cause less astonishment than if I make them vanish myself!"

So Stephen did, and was then shown into the cottage, which held but one room, barely furnished with a low bed, a rough table and bench, and a cooking-fire, almost out. Rollo bade him take his own humble pallet, while he bedded himself down on the rushes that littered the floor, wrapped in a cloak. The traveller did not protest, both because he was weary enough to welcome a little comfort, and because he did not wish to offend his host.

The harness, saddle and rich saddlecloth they concealed under straw in the corner, for, as Rollo said, "There's many a rogue around these parts who would kill a man without a second thought to get such fine tackle for his own mount! And what of your steed, sir, how will we take care of him while we sleep, for he is an even greater prize? He may come in with us; the door has a stout bar, but it will leave us crowded."

"Nay, Rollo, my friend, do not fret; this horse is more than a match for any sneak-thief who prowls at night!", and from outside he heard the horse laugh his agreement.

Little did any of the three realise just how soon this confidence would be put to the test.

Chapter Four

Stephen awoke from a deep sleep less than two hours after midnight; he was alert immediately; his experience as a ship's captain had given him that ability, so necessary at sea. He listened for what had disturbed him, and heard a low muttering, heavy but cautious steps, and a faint clinking that could have been harness or weapons. There seemed to be several men outside, and he could sense that they were at the sides as well as before the cottage.

He heard Rollo stir, and then whisper, "Say nothing, sir, lest they know we wake; they may grow careless if they believe we are still snoring. Besides, they will expect me to be alone here, unless they are foreigners."

Both men drew on their boots; neither had taken off any clothes to go to bed. Rollo went to the door to peer out through the narrow space at its edge, but as he did there came a thundering knock upon the door, which startled him so that he called out "Who's there?" before thinking.

"So ye're awake, stout Rollo!" came a cry, "Open up to the King's Guard; we would know of strangers passing this night."

"Is it you, Master Wilkins, then?" said Rollo, recognizing the voice, "Give me a moment to get dressed, for I have no wish to freeze my shanks!"

Turning to Stephen, he motioned him to hide behind the bed; it was not high enough to go under. As Stephen crouched by the wall, Rollo leant the straw pallet against him so he could not easily be seen. It was well that he did, because, as he opened the door, the man outside shone the beam of a horn lantern around the room; it was only lit by a candle, but in that gloom it penetrated like a shaft of daylight.

Then Rollo pushed the lantern-bearer back as he stepped out, and the door swung to behind him.

"Who are these strangers you seek, Wilkins? I have seen no-one on the road since the sergeant left last morning, and as you know it takes a very cunning man to slip past me. Why, I heard you all, the moment you came up the track, blundering along like a trample of oxen."

"We were told of a lone horseman, spotted by the King's shepherd from the top of the downs, who gave us the news as soon as he drove his flock back into the domain at nightfall. He was seen to enter the forest on your road, Rollo, so if he didn't pass here he must still be on the loose among the trees. Are you sure you saw no-one?"

"Do you see him or his horse here, then, or any sign of them?" Rollo retorted, speaking as though stung by the disbelief of the guard in his diligence. At this, Stephen's heart dropped; what if the men were provoked into searching for him or his horse there and then? And where was the magical steed? Was he hiding, or had he taken his leave?

"I meant no offence," said the guard, "you know we are charged to be painstaking in our duties. Of course we saw no horse nearby; we searched all around before we knocked on your door. I'm satisfied, and we'll soon be off; we'll cast about to either side as we make our way back to the town. But there is one more matter I would raise with you before we depart."

Once again, Stephen, crouching behind the bed, felt his anxiety rise, gripping his chest so that he almost cried out. He wondered for an instant whether he should reveal himself and make a clean breast of his situation; he had no quarrel with the King or his men, but he decided that Rollo must have had a reason for all this secrecy, and he had no reason to distrust him, he seemed a decent man.

The guard continued, "You are getting idle and slack, my fine Rollo; I have a mind to report you for your failure to the King!" but then, as Rollo started to protest, "Nay, nay, my friend, I am jesting with thee! But you should know that along the road as we came, by the black rocks where old Abel dwelt ten years ago, the stream has found its way across the road again; the gully needs filling in before Master Swine-belly's horse stumbles in it a second time and throws him into the ditch!"

His companions all laughed and jeered at this; Stephen gathered that whoever he might be, this Swine-belly, he was not well regarded in this company.

And then, as Stephen could hear, the guard and his troop mounted their horses and set off, with shouts of farewell to Rollo, who returned their banter and then shut and barred the door before letting out a great breath of relief.

"I'll tell you freely, my lord, I had my heart in my mouth more times than I liked during that business! But where has your horse taken himself?" Stephen had no chance to reply as he straightened up from his hiding place, before there was a whinny from outside. He hastened to open the door again, and there stood his steed, complete with harness, saddle and trappings, whose silver buckles caught the light of the moon, now in full sail above the trees around the glade.

"Mount quickly, sir, we must catch up the guards!" said the horse, and Stephen had no choice but to snatch up his knapsack and do that, bewildered though he was. "I have to go now, Rollo," he called to his astonished host, "I hope I will see you again soon, and then I can tell you what is to befall me next, for now I know not. I thank you for your comfort and your support."

With that, the horse soon broke once again into an easy canter, across the glade, down the track and back onto the road.

Chapter Five

Very soon they heard the hoofbeats and jingling of the troop ahead, and could see the flare of the torches that the leading riders were using to light their way; the moon could not penetrate to the road, for it wound closely through clumps of holly and blackthorn bushes that were now growing densely to either side.

The horse turned his head, saying, "Do not be concerned about how you will be treated by the guards, my lord; they will not see you - or rather, they will see you, but each will take you for one or another of his fellows. We need to be in their company in order to pass the town gate, for my magic can not help us in that. I will tell you the reason later."

Sure enough, there was no reaction from any of the guards as Stephen and his mount joined them, and very quickly they all fell into a steady but swift pace which took them through forest that was becoming more open, with great oak and beech trees over a grassy undergrowth. Morning was coming, and the leading riders threw away their torches on the road. About an hour and a half after they had left the cottage, the troop emerged from the forest altogether, and Stephen could see that the road, wider now, led down a long slope to a walled town, layered with mist and early morning smoke, but visible enough so that he could tell that it was of substantial size. Beyond the roofs of the houses rose up the ramparts and battlements of a great castle, built on a green mound.

The town gate was still shut, and the chief guard dismounted, went up to the huge stone pillar on the left and pealed a bell the size of a bucket which hung there. As soon as the gatekeeper looked through the iron grille in the oaken door, he recognised the guards; Stephen and his unwitting companions heard the sound of heavy bars being withdrawn and then the doors swung slowly outwards. But before they could enter the town, they had to wait for a herd of sheep to be driven out, followed by goatherds and goose-girls with their flocks, and another cackling crowd, this time of washerwomen, headed with their tubs of linen for the rocky banks of a stream which lay a hundred yards off to the side of the road.

Apparently it took more than a mob of animals and humble workers to persuade the gatekeeper to bestir himself to open the gates before he was ready; but he was affable and lively enough as he exchanged gossip with the guard troopers. Stephen thought to himself that gatekeepers everywhere, like innkeepers, are always rich sources of information, even if much it might be based on rumour, bragging or even sheer mischief.

Once remounted, the guard captain and his men spurred their mounts and made off at a fast trot up the main street, a cobbled lane barely wide enough for three horses abreast, which seemed to lead in the direction of the castle. Stephen's horse did not follow, instead he turned off into an alley that ran parallel to the town wall; he pulled up, and Stephen dismounted and took his head, so he might talk to him.

"I twice promised you some explanations," said the horse, "but so far there has hardly been a chance to give them. If you will permit me, I will change my shape again, and we can go and take some breakfast while I relate all that I need to tell you. Please close your eyes for a moment; I know that you, a seafaring man, have a strong stomach, but it is very upsetting to see a horse dissolve into another form!"

Stephen did as he was bid, but in only a few seconds he heard the horse say, in a voice that was strangely different, but still recognisable, "You may open your eyes now."

When he looked about him, it took a moment for him to grasp that he now had for a companion a young boy, maybe twelve or thirteen years old, dressed like a squire in padded jerkin and woollen hose, who was nodding and smiling at him. He took Stephen's hand, and led him along the alley to a tiny shop where a spare but rosy-cheeked woman with twinkling eyes waved them in to sit down.

"Is it a good breakfast you'll be wanting, young sirs?" she said. "I can offer you bread and honey and milk fresh from my nanny-goat, but I have no meats this morning, because ..."

Here she hesitated, and decided to say no more.

Stephen thought that he had better be the one to speak up; it might appear strange if the lad took charge, "Why thank you, dame," he said, "that will suit us well. To tell the truth we could make a meal out of turnip-tops this morning!"

They sat on a bench against the window, which had no glass, and the woman set wooden platters before them on a table that, though small, almost filled the room. She disappeared through a doorway hung with a curtain of sacking, and returned almost at once with a round loaf which steamed as Stephen broke it open, and a bowl of honey into which he and the boy dipped the crusts of bread. She went again into the back room and brought back a pitcher of milk and a basket of small new apples.

"These are the first of the season," she said, "but they are sweet even if they are, by rights, too small to be picked. I would not offer them to all my customers, but a growing boy ...", and she pinched the lad's cheek and chuckled, then left them alone to enjoy their meal.

When they had eaten their fill of bread and honey, Stephen took an apple and looked expectantly towards the boy, who smiled and said, "No doubt you are impatient to hear my story; it will take several sittings to relate, so I will start by explaining how I came by my powers." He turned round, knelt on the bench and, poking his head out of the window, looked up and down the alley. Then he sat again and began his tale, talking in a low tone which was quite audible to Stephen as they sat together, but would have been hard to hear by anyone else; the shop woman was now standing in the alley gossiping with her neighbours.

"You may ask what is my true form, my lord; am I a horse masquerading as a boy, or a boy who can become a horse for a while? The answer is both and neither, but the surest truth is that now my form is less important to me than my mission. I am the servant of a great sage and magician who has sworn his enmity to those who would seize power without right. He is so implacably convinced that power itself is evil, that he has forbidden me to use my magic to do any more than deceive the ungodly; or even the just, if needs be. I can not, and he will not, harm anyone in any way, even if this forbearance means that they might prevail in their ill-doing."

He paused, and threw an apple-core out of the window, causing a fluttering and a squawking as the hens in the alley fought over it. Stephen said nothing, but leant even closer to his companion. The boy went on.

"I first made myself into a tiny winged horse for two reasons: to come up on you unnoticed, and then to convince you quickly that I was magical. I then became a true horse (except for the speaking!) because a horse is universally regarded by men as being noble and trustworthy; if I had taken the form of a bear, or even of a dog, you might have feared me or seen me as hostile. If I had shown myself to you as a human, you would have needed long explanations of myself and of my quest; but you trusted me as a horse at once, is that not so? When the guards came in the night, I became an owl, sitting on a branch, watching and listening, but you never saw me thus."

Stephen's head was spinning, but underneath all his confusion, he felt growing there a sense of relief, a promise of calm to come, and the beginnings of joyful excitement. All these emotions were helping to lift the suffocating blanket of despair that had overwhelmed him since he had first realised his loved ones had been taken from him. He had so many questions to ask, but he was himself surprised by what first came to his lips. "What is it you and your master want of me, for I am ready to serve you at once?" he cried, with such longing that he did not think to keep down his voice.

The shopkeeper, startled by his outburst, stepped back inside asking if all was well with them, but Stephen regained his composure and assured her that there was nothing amiss. At that, she collected up the mugs and platters and asked, "Can I bring the gentlemen anything more? I have a fine honey-cake that I baked yesterday, or I can go and fetch something else from the market, you have but to say."

The boy answered her, "No more, thank you, dame. But if we are not driving your customers away, we would like to stay and talk for a while; your house is a pleasant spot for sitting and chatting. Later we will ask you if you know of a place where we might lodge for a few days; we have many matters to attend to in the town."

As she disappeared into the back room, he turned to Stephen, "I will soon answer your question, my lord, but I believe that there is more you need to understand before you are ready for that. Maybe there are some other things that puzzle you now, or shall I go on with the tale as it comes to me?"

Stephen hastened to assure him that he would be more patient. "But first," he added, "tell me what I should call you; do you have a name, or is that as fleeting as your form?"

The boy laughed merrily, and took Stephen's hand. "My baptismal name is Christopher, and I use it whenever I am in human form. Since beasts have no language, they have no names for each other, so if I become one again, you must simply call me 'horse', or 'wolf' or 'spider', whatever you see! My name is Christopher, but family and friends call me Kit."

Just then, there was a commotion in the alley outside, and the sound of people running, and calling to each other as they ran: "Is it the King?", "It's the King and his knights, riding out in a regiment!", "What's afoot, is the enemy at our gates?", "Keep aside, keep aside!", "To the castle green!" and so on. Kit motioned Stephen to follow him, and they stepped into the lane to join the throng making their way up the main street.

Chapter Six

Stephen made to offer a silver coin to the shop-woman, who was standing by the door, craning this way and that, to see what was going on, but she refused it, saying, "Have you no coppers, sir? I cannot give you change now, but you will pay me when you see me again, I'm sure; you are not like those ..."; and she stopped herself with a grimace once more.

The two made their way with the crowd, swept along almost willy-nilly, until they had gone the length of the main street and were in an open place or market square, alongside a green which bordered the castle moat. There they indeed found a cohort of a score or more of men mounted on war-horses, both riders and horses dressed in mail, the knights in helms and wearing gauntlets. They were drawn up in front of a low stone-built stage fronting the green, upon which was set a wooden dais, draped in swags and bunting, with standards fluttering on staffs at the corners.

On the dais stood an impressive figure, armoured all in black, with the red cross of the crusades on his surcoat; the King himself. As Stephen and the lad took a stand on a slight rise, an attendant raised a staff, and the crowd grew suddenly silent. King Arnold began to speak, raising his visor so that he could be heard and seen more easily.

"People of Woodhampton town, I greet you warmly; you are among the most loyal of my subjects and have always supported me gladly and made me welcome on my visits. In recent months this has been especially welcome, for we have come into difficult times, as you all know. We are threatened as we have not been for more than twenty years, but if it were only our old enemies, we could withstand them with ease."

"The threat that now looms over us is not one that yields to force of arms alone; we will need all our skill and fortitude to combat it, yes, but we will also have to call upon deep and strange forces to stand against the evil that has been unleashed against us by I know not who. I do know that my ungodly cousin, Prince Gerald of the Wilderness, will seize upon any defeat that we suffer and turn it to his own ends, but he has never had either the ability or the courage to enlist such dark allies himself."

20

A hubbub arose from the crowd; men grasped their neighbours by the arm or shoulders, women threw their aprons over their faces; some folk cried defiance, others wailed in despair. Stephen could judge as he looked about him that there was no great sense of surprise among them, rather almost a feeling of relief, together with a mingling of fear and eagerness for action. The King raised his arm and there was an instant hush; those at the back stood on tip-toe and craned to get a better look as he spoke again.

"You see with me my knights, some of whom came with me to the Holy Land; they are all valiant and experienced in battle, many have proved their worth at my side; they are loyal to the last man, but they and I are all helpless unless we can seek out who or what is the source of this scourge."

There was a renewed babble from the crowd. Several of the knights turned their faces away in shame, others stood with their heads bowed. In the front rank a massive bearded warrior paled, swayed and leant forward in his saddle, covering his face with his gauntlets, overcome with the shame and frustration of the moment.

Again the King spoke, turning towards his men. "Blame not yourselves, my faithful friends, nor should anyone hold you in contempt. What we face now may be an unearthly enemy, against which even valour and strength will not prevail. All we know is that it is indeed evil, for it has caused many evil events these last two months."

"Listen to the words of my wisest adviser, Musgrave, who will tell you what we know for certain, for there are so many tales and rumours among the people of the castle and of the town that no two people have the same story of what has been happening."

With that, the King stepped back, and gave his place on the stage to a tall figure, a woman. Stephen leaned forward to make her out better. She was dressed in a abbess's robes of brown wool, but with her head uncovered and the hood thrown back, and leant stooping on a tall, crooked staff held in her right hand. She had long, matted white hair and appeared very old, but when she spoke, her voice rang out vigorously and clearly, so that even those at the back of the throng could hear every word.

"Who among you has not heard of strange happenings these last weeks?" she started, and there was a stirring and a muttering in

21

the crowd. "I was told this morning, by the lad who brings the water, that his mother's goat spoke to him last night, telling him that he should shed all his clothes and run to the woods! What do you think of that, my friends? I told him not to go yet, until he was told the same by at least a cow, better a horse!"

A ripple of laughter ran through the crowd, but it was uneasy laughter and died away almost immediately. As Stephen glanced left and right, he could see that there was a weight pressing on the townsfolk's hearts and minds; their faces were strained and they wanted desperately to hear more.

The tall woman began again. "That could ha' been fancy and dreaming; he was but a lad. But there are other tales I've heard about that knot up my innards; vanishings there've been, and things have changed in ways they shouldn't, and people have seen things in broad daylight with not a sup of ale to help them. I myself, two days since, saw the table in my chamber walk over to the window and peer out, as if it was looking at the weather. When I cried out, it stopped, but there it was, ten feet from its place, with the dusty marks of its feet still showing where it had stood before."

Over to his left Stephen saw the dame who had given them breakfast; she was waving a rag, wanting the speaker to see her. She did, and pointed to her, saying, "Speak up, Mistress, let us all hear your tale, too."

She covered her face with her apron for a moment, but then spoke out in a voice that quavered a little but still could be heard well enough. "Oh, my lady, I've wanted to tell of this for near a week, but was afeared to, lest I be locked up as a madwoman or taken for a witch. Many around will know me, I keep a little eating-house for travellers and those with no hearth of their own. So my larder is kept stocked against chance of visitors, with bread, and cabbage and roots and fruit, and hams and bacon and sometimes the sausages that Mistress Triggs makes over by the west wall."

There was a call from a tall powerful-looking man at the edge of the throng as she drew breath, "Get on with it, Martha, we know all that", and she again threw her apron over her face, bobbing forward a couple of times in agitation; but she regained her calm and went on.

22

"Well, I'll come to it then. Last Tuesday, or was it Wednesday? No it'd be Tuesday, because I allus goes to the stream to wash my aprons of a Wednesday. Well, I had a couple of pedlars call in for a bite; I've served them before, they're honest men, not like some as I could tell you of, and they needed a good feed of meat. Well, I went to my larder, it's at the back of my place, in the thick of the town wall, it never gets too warm there, except when we gets those dog days sometimes ..."

People in the crowd were getting impatient, and there was a muttering and a shuffling as they waited for her to get to the point, but there seemed to be a general agreement among them that she should not be interrupted again.

"... anyway, I lifted up the damp linen I keep over the crocks of cold roast meat and bacon and such, and it had all turned to stone! It looked the same as it allus does, but when I touched it, it was as hard as iron! I tried it with my teeth, I did; I've still got most on em, old as I be, but never a mark could I make on any of it, hard as I tried! And everyone who's come into my place since then has had to make do with bread and other vittles, because never a bit of meat have I had since then, nor will I till I can gather some more coppers."

As she finished, several man and women in the crowd were emboldened by her example, and called out their experiences, which ranged from merely unusual tales of the same kind as hers - clothing transformed into wood, wine which billowed out of flasks as purple smoke as soon as the stopper was loosed, disappearances of household items, houses invaded by beetles or hedgehogs - to chilling accounts of a more evil kind. One young ploughboy had come home at nightfall to find his father, mother and sister all struck dumb and witless; there had been unexplained sudden deaths of farm animals, and a distraught woman had told of a kitten found in a crib, dressed in the swaddling of her missing two-day old baby. As she haltingly related this chilling story, the crowd grew still and silent.

Stephen felt his own grief and loss rising once again; in all the excitement he had thrust them away, but they were too profound to ignore for long. But he now felt strangely comforted that he was not alone, for he was convinced that he was the victim of the same mysterious forces that had brought about the bizarre happenings in the town. The great wave that had taken his family was certainly nothing like any that he had seen before in all his seafaring experience.

The tall figure on the dais spoke again, "Thank you, good people, for your tales. I'll warrant there's many another that could be related here if we but had more time; am I right, my friends?" But the mood for sharing experiences seemed to have disappeared, and though some in the crowd nodded, they remained speechless as the King's advisor held up her staff in both hands.

"So we all know that there is evil abroad, do we not? His Majesty has said that his cousin Gerald is an enemy, and cursed besides, but the King and I believe that he has no real sway over these forces of darkness. It would be a straight task to capture or kill him and his band, we have brave men enough, but this would not solve the riddle; the hounds of Hell have been slipped by now and they are crazed by the scent of their prey and are out of human control. Before we can do more, we must find out what it is we are to deal with."

There was a ragged cheer from the gathering as she finished speaking and stood back, but Stephen sensed that the townsfolk were shaken by the realisation that they were dealing not with a few isolated incidents but a concerted onslaught. Near where he and his young companion stood, he could see more than one woman weeping in terror, and men who twisted their hands together in frustration, not knowing whether to stay or to return to their homes.

Chapter Seven

The King stepped to the front of the stage and began talking; his voice was now low, but the crowd was so intent that they heard every word.

"My people," he said, "I must go now to ride to my other towns and enlist their help as I have sought yours. I know that they, like you, are loyal, and I will enjoin them and you to hold yourselves ready. I have no orders for you yet, for we have no plan of campaign; all that I have learnt about warfare is of no value to us now. When I return, I will select a few from among you to join a council which will meet in the capital city ten days hence; with those wise folk from my other towns we shall sit together and take stock of our resources. For now, fare you well!"

With that, he mounted his charger, which had been led near to the front of the stage, then with his knights following in a brave display of raised lances and trumpet calls, passed through a second town gate at the end of the wall near the castle moat, and headed off up a broad carriage road which skirted the town. A scattered group of boys and young children ran behind the troop excitedly for a while, and then returned to the marketplace as the King and his men disappeared into the woods and were lost to view.

Stephen felt his sleeve tugged, and turned to find what his young companion wanted.

"Come now, my lord, and we will go to meet my master. Together, we have much to discuss before the King returns; you are already selected for his council and you must be prepared!"

As Stephen opened his mouth to ask what he meant, Kit shook his head and put his finger to his lips, and, taking his hand, led him back into the streets of the town.

The ways were busy with townspeople returning to their homes and work places, and Stephen and his guide made slow progress, twisting and turning through the maze of streets until the lad suddenly stopped in an open space, not much more than a widening of the street in front of a church. Glancing around to make sure no-one was paying particular attention, he drew Stephen into the narrow alley beside the church, taking him to a low door which opened to a flight of dusty worn steps leading downward.

As Kit pulled the door to behind them they were engulfed in complete darkness, but Kit, who seemed to be familiar with the surroundings, took Stephens hand and guided him, saying, "Here is a high step; now we go left; watch for the roof, it lowers here," and so on.

In a few minutes Stephen heard another door being opened, and saw that there was now a faint and flickering light, which revealed a long, level passage, its walls green with moss and glistening wet. The light came from rush-lights fixed in sconces at intervals along the way.

As the pair walked on, the air grew colder and still colder; Stephen guessed that they must be striking deep into the mountain behind the town, but he refrained from asking his guide questions as they walked, trusting that an explanation would be given in good time. After what must have been nearly half an hour, they saw ahead of them another door; heavy, studded with iron bolts and covered, like everything else, with damp green moss. Kit picked up a heavy stone and struck twice on the door, making a heavy boom that echoed along the passage.

After only a few heartbeats, the door swung open, and a shaft of light almost blinded Stephen, whose eyes had accommodated to the gloom. Kit led him forward and they stepped into a huge cavern, lit by thousands of candles, like a cathedral, whose roof disappeared in the dark above. Standing in the centre of the space, on a tiled floor of black and white squares, like a chessboard, was a group of three figures.

Kit thrust Stephen forward, whispering, "Fear not, they are my master and his trusted allies," and he walked slowly but steadily forward until he could see them clearly.

At the centre of the group was a man of medium height, slightly shorter than Stephen, with a balding head and grey-streaked beard and moustache, dressed in a long tunic of richly-embroidered linen and a blue cloak with white fur edging. He held out his hand and spoke in a powerful but high-pitched voice, "Welcome, Captain Stephen, we have work to do together, and you will play an important part which you cannot yet

26

imagine. You will recognise one of my companions and the other is my brother Osric. My name is Vincent, but most call me simply the Beeman."

Turning to Kit, who had moved forward to join the group, he went on, "Thank you, Kit, my boy, for bringing us our new ally. As usual you have served me well."

Stephen saw that, indeed, standing on the Bee-Man's left, was Musgrave, the tall woman who had been introduced by the King as his chief adviser. He wondered how she had managed to get here before Kit and himself, but once again trusted that all his questions would be answered in due course.

Chapter Eight

Vincent, the Beeman, stepped forward and grasped Stephen's hand, gently but firmly. "First, I must ask you whether you agree to join us in this venture; I will not ask any man to undertake any task that he can not commit himself to whole-heartedly in free will. I cannot tell you what perils we will face together, but you have already observed that our adversary, whatever form he or it may take, is truly malevolent."

"Let we four, and our young friend, withdraw to my counsel chamber and we shall share whatever each of us knows, to prepare ourselves for planning our next moves. When the King returns, he will bring others who will join with us in this enterprise, but we should not delay our conference, for I feel we have little enough time to plan as it is."

He led the way through a door draped in heavy tapestry into a room where there was a long table; he seated himself at the centre of one side, with Musgrave on his left and Osric on his right, placing Kit and Stephen on the other side of the table. A man dressed in the clothes of a monk, carrying a parchment, a quill, a small pad of paper and an inkhorn took his place beside Stephen.

"We all have knowledge of strange, even terrible, events; some directly, others related by witnesses," said Vincent, "let each of us recount what is known for certain, and William, our scrivener here, will record it all, so we may all be sure of what we are discussing. I fear that if we are not meticulous, we may be led astray in flights of unruly conjecture. First, let me call on Stephen, our guest."

Stephen drew his thoughts together and, as calmly as he could, told of the events of his shipwreck in the order in which they had happened: the calm night, his ship sailing steadily before a fair wind, making her assigned course; the sudden wave rising up before him until it towered seemingly almost to the sky; and then the overwhelming crash as the solid mass of water fell upon the ship. How he found himself rising to the surface from the depths, after an interminable period during which he thought himself drowned and dead. How he searched around, calling for anyone to answer, and how, hearing and seeing no-one, he struck out toward the sound of waves pounding on the rocky coast, for the wind, if wind there had been, was now quietened.

At that point in his story, he stopped, saying "… from then on, there was nothing unnatural - at least until Kit appeared - at first I took him for a bee!" He paused a moment and then almost blurted out "By the by, Sir, if it not be an impertinent question, why is it that you are called 'The Beeman'?"

Vincent chuckled, then said "Never fear to speak up in this company, we are all intent on solving this vile puzzle, and we must not hold back any scrap of our thoughts. I am called the Beeman because that is what I was; a humble bee-keeper. Many's the jar of honey that I have sold at our local market, and many's the jar I have given away to those who needed it. But that occupation is also the key to my present calling, for it was during the long hours I spent tending my hives and observing the ways of the bees that I became fully aware of the strange powers that I had had since childhood. I shall tell you more of this when we have not such urgent business to deal with."

He then called on each of the group in turn to relate what they knew about the frightening changes that had been happening over the last ten days. Stephen was surprised to hear that most of them were so recent; having only just arrived, he had assumed them to be well-established.

Musgrave and Osric told of events that were similar in kind to those Stephen had already heard about on the castle green, and Kit held back, looking at Vincent as though to imply that he what he himself might contribute would not be as important as what his master would say.

Vincent had been listening intently, from time to time murmuring to the scrivener to take special note of one thing or another, or to point out that an account related was not first-hand and might be better listed as a rumour, but now he stood up and placed his hand on his brother's shoulder.

Osric got to his feet and started to speak, in a strangely high-pitched but musical voice. "While I have been listening, I have been trying to twist these bits and pieces this way and that, to see whether they can be arranged into a meaningful pattern, together with what I know from my own observations. I am now going to present to you the skeleton of a story, clothed here and there in rags and tatters. Maybe we together can put some flesh on it and see whether it is of any help to us or not; whether it will reveal any vulnerability that we can seize upon to fight it with, for fight we must."

"Some of these weird happenings may be designed to confuse us, to throw us off the scent; others may be vital elements that our unknown assailant has been forced to let slip, and, of course, there may be more and worse to come."

"I will tell you all what I think, and you must challenge me at any point if you disagree or have questions. Above all, do not defer to me; I may be more experienced or wiser than some of you, but not by much!"

"Then, our scrivener will list again what he has been noting down, and my good Kit will write a note on each item of no more than two or three words, on a page from this pad. Then we can arrange these notes this way and that, to see whether that will help our thinking."

I will not risk boring my readers with a detailed account of the discussions that followed; after Osric had given his account, the six talked and disputed for over four hours, breaking off for a while halfway through, to have a bite to eat and a cup to sip, and to walk about in thought.

Finally, Vincent called them back to the table. After a great deal of shuffling and rearrangement, the notes had finished up in three piles, two small and one much larger. Indicating the latter, he said "As we have decided, many of these tales are no more than interesting; they do not threaten us in any more than trifling ways; all they tell us is that our unknown adversaries are adept in the magical arts. But changing meat into stone, or clothing into wood, or wine into smoke are but fairground tricks for our amusement, and if it were not for the other strange events, we could dismiss them. Well, we will dismiss them, for now anyway, and turn our attention to these other more serious matters."

"This pile must concern us more, because the trickeries that are listed on these pages are more dangerous. If animals can be made to speak, or furniture to move about by itself, or great waves to arise, these beasts or these objects can be used as agents against us, and it might be very difficult to defend ourselves against such fighters that do not have the characters or perhaps even the weaknesses of men. We must include these hazards in our planning, so far as we are able, and we must set to so as to discover how these transformations have been brought about, and by who or what."

"But it is this third pile of notes that worries me the most. If a baby can be turned into a kitten, then a man or woman can, likewise, be changed into who knows what. If a person can be struck dumb or senseless, or even be made to vanish, how can we deal with that? How can we prevent such evils?"

Now Musgrave rose to speak; she had taken full part in the discussions, but now she drew herself up and, starting quietly and then becoming more forceful, spoke:

"I have no quarrel with what Vincent has just said; he has put his finger on much that is important. However, we must not forget that there are more stages that we must pass through before we can even think of taking action. First, we need to wait for the King to return, bringing with him those he has recruited to this campaign. They may have grasped the task differently from us, and we may see things in a new light when we have heard what notions they bring with them."

"Secondly, we must realise that we do not yet have any inkling of the nature of our opponent; we can, yes, list what has been done, what weapons have been used against us, but we do not know who or what has caused them, nor do we know the reasons for them. It may be that they are mere mischief; like the playful acts of children who do not realise the harm that are causing. Or they may be a more sinister form of play, as by a sorcerer who is trying out his or her powers, simply to test them or to keep from getting bored, heedless of their effect."

"What I fear most," went on the tall woman, becoming even more stern, "is that it is the harm that is being done to us and ours that is the ultimate motive; that we are being attacked by an adversary determined to bring us low, or destroy us absolutely, either all of us, or only a group of key people."

At this point, Vincent thanked Musgrave and drew attention to the lateness of the hour. "We shall sleep now, and in the morning continue. It may be that the King will have sent a messenger by then, to tell us of his progress. Good night, my friends, we shall break our fast early tomorrow and then see what befalls."

Chapter Nine

Stephen slept very soundly that night; he could hardly even remember being shown to his room, sinking gratefully into a feather bed and covering himself with woollen blankets - after his previous night under a bush this was luxury indeed.

In the morning he was wakened by a smiling serving maid, who wished him good morrow, and brought a jug of hot water and a basin. She went out, and soon returned with fresh clothing, more presentable than his own well-worn and dusty garments. He had slept in a nightshirt he had found on the bed.

"When you are ready, my lord, breakfast is being taken in the kitchen, below this room – we do not stand on ceremony here, and all eat together, whatever our station; the master would have it no other way."

When he had washed and dressed, Stephen went over to the window and threw back the shutters. The sun streamed in, and he was surprised to see that the room overlooked a wide terrace, with gardens and shrubberies that led away to woods, beyond a high wall. He had assumed that the entire house was subterranean, for until then he had seen no windows, but he saw now that it was built into the hillside.

He found his way down to the kitchen, already full of shouts and laughter, and was greeted by Osric and Kit, who were finishing their porridge and washing it down with, on the one hand, ale, and on the other, milk. There was no sign of Musgrave or Vincent.

There was lively conversation among all present, and more tales of strange happenings and dire predictions of disasters to come, but Stephen sensed that behind the anxieties that were expressed, there was general confidence that right would prevail, and that King Arnold and his knights, with Vincent, Musgrave and their supporters, would ultimately solve the mystery.

Stephen had just started wondering what he should do next, when Vincent at last appeared, bursting into the room, with his expression frantic and his mouth in a rictus of despair.

"Did I not say that there might today be a message from the King?" he blurted out when he could finally control himself, "Well, I was right, but I can feel no satisfaction about my prediction, for the message is of nothing good and everything evil – the King is wounded and is being brought here on a horse-litter, and half his men are dead! I was told this not a minute ago, by my trusted messenger."

"He and his knights had gone but a few leagues from here yesterday, when they were suddenly engulfed in a noxious fog or smoke, which rolled out of the woods like a horde of ghosts. And while they were sightless and lost in it, they were set upon by what some who saw it have called a river of rats. Oh, may God help us, I never thought it would get so bad so soon!"

"Let my messenger tell you more!" He led forward a young girl, no more than nine or ten, who stepped up on a foot-stool and began:

"I often bear messages for the Beeman, and yesterday he enjoined me to accompany King Arnold and his knights, that I might report on whatever I saw that might be important for Vincent to know. I took the form of a pigeon, and it was easy to keep up with them; from time to time I would fly ahead, still in eyeshot, and rest my wings a little. As it happened, this habit was what saved me from the fate that befell the main party. I have to beware of hawks, for whom a fat young pigeon is a satisfying meal; I always carry a token of my master, and most hawks acknowledge it, and even give me assistance when it is needed."

"We had been travelling but a few hours when the road, which had dwindled to a rough track, but was still serviceable for horse traffic, entered a large wood, known to the locals as the bluebell wood. King Arnold and his men plunged into it without hesitation; I have heard that those who live nearby are not as eager, since there are many tales told about its dangers. I flew past the party until I came to a clearing, and perched on a high branch to wait for them to catch up. I had lost sight of them, and for this dereliction of my duty I am truly remorseful, although it may have saved my life."

"As I peered back along the track, which was closely crowded in by trees and bushes, I heard a sound which somehow chilled me to the core — it was like the distant rushing of a mountain stream, but it was mixed with sad, yearning moans, as though something or someone was gravely afeared. And then I saw the mist, or smoke, billowing along the track and out into the clearing. I knew not what to do, so I held my place on the branch and waited."

"And then it came; a river, not of water, but made of a mass of wriggling bodies. I could not make out their separate shapes, they were massed together so. The closest I can get to telling it was that they were like rats, and about that size. This river crossed the clearing, and their noise rose to a scream. Had I been equipped with fingers, I would have stopped my ears. In a few minutes they had gone, along the far track and away."

Chapter Ten

As the messenger finished, Vincent lifted her down from the stool and kissed her forehead, "Thank you, my little Belinda, I will relate the rest of what you told me."

"When my little pigeon was sure that the rat-swarm had indeed gone, she flew back bravely along the track. What she saw then seemed at first like a charnel house; men and horses all lying in disarray, and she thought there were none left alive. She flew down and resumed her human shape, for there was no longer any need for flying, and she wished to see whether she could give aid, or at least say a prayer over the corpses."

Vincent bowed his head and wept a little, "What a dutiful, beautiful child she is!" Then he drew himself up again.

"As she proceeded with her sombre duties, for those of the company who seemed clearly to be dead, to her astonishment and delight, some who she had taken to be corpses started, one by one, to arouse themselves, as though from a stupor or feverish sleep. She cried out joyfully, and the first of them to stir asked her where they were, and what had befallen. As she started to explain, they shook themselves awake, and she could see that they were beginning to remember."

"Those who woke first attended to the truly dead, and then turned to those slow to arouse themselves, and a hubbub of questions and guesses began. But then they saw that the King, in his distinctive armour, was still unconscious, so two of the knights carefully removed his helm and sponged his face with water from a flask. He at last opened his eyes and grimaced in pain, saying that his legs were injured. And indeed, once his greaves and cuisses were unbuckled and taken off, they could see that both legs had been crushed. They then realised that his steed had fallen upon him and that the steel croupiere that protected its hind-quarters had been what caused his injury."

"As some attended to the horses, and others buried and blessed their dead companions, two of the knights cut stout saplings and, with surcoats and saddle-cloths fashioned a litter that was fastened to the stirrup leathers of two horses, one before and one behind. Then they started back here, but at a slow walk only, because even though they had bound the King's legs to splints,

36

he was still in acute pain, and cried out at every jolt; brave man though he be."

"Belinda began at first to walk with them, and they told her that the smoke or fog had overcome them all, so the whole company, horses and all, had fallen into a stupor. She then excused herself, became a pigeon once more and flew here to tell this history. Taking account of the time they took to reach the wood and making allowances for the delay and the slowness of their progress, they are still some hours away. They are very wise to remain together; who knows what further attacks may be made on them!"

Stephen joined in with the general buzz of talk that followed these accounts; then, after a while, finding that he was standing with Kit, decided to ask about something that had been intriguing him, "Tell me, Kit, are all Vincent's helpers who can change their shape young boys and girls?"

Kit nodded, saying "You have guessed right, Captain Stephen; yes that is so. When I start growing the first fluff of my beard, I shall lose that power, and when Belinda starts becoming a woman, she will no longer be able to change. This is the law — I know not whether it is a law made by Vincent, or by a higher authority in the magical world. You could ask him yourself; he keeps no secrets."

Stephen found the day dragging, although he was busy enough; he was introduced to everyone, he was shown round the castle, both Vincent's domain and the upper halls and apartments where the King lodged with all his staff. He found that Musgrave (who he now found out was a noblewoman, Lady Beatrice de Gonville-Musgrave, and by rights should have been addressed as "Your Ladyship", but disdained this) had her own suite and staff, as befitted the King's chief adviser.

All were uneasy, and found themselves from time to time going to a window and straining to see along the road from the woods. No-one could settle until they could greet the King and his remaining knights and find out how they were and what they knew.

Mid-way through the afternoon, a lad came and found Stephen and asked him to come to Vincent's counsel chamber, where he found Vincent, Osric, Musgrave, Kit and little Belinda, already seated around the table, with the scrivener, William, in attendance.

"Now, Captain and friends," said Vincent, "what we must do now is plan our next moves; matters have changed, and if we do not take stock before the King and his diminished retinue arrive, we could lose track. His Majesty will be in no condition for talking until he has been nursed back to some degree of health, but we will be subjected to an onslaught of half-remembered incidents and opinions hastily formed, from the knights, no doubt. If we do not try to gather our old and new evidence together soon, we shall plunge deeper into confusion and puzzlement."

"We think we know what injured the King, but was the fall from the horse all that assailed him?

And what of those brave dead knights? What killed them, they could not all have broken their necks falling from their steeds, could they? And we must make full use of the fact that we have, for the very first time, seen our enemy, or at least his or its manifestation, in the form of the so-called rats - what part did they play in all these extraordinary happenings?"

Chapter Eleven

Stephen rose, somewhat hesitantly, "Forgive me if I put forward a suggestion, and the company may tell me if it be worth pursuing. What if we visit the place where these terrible events happened, before - may the Lord forgive me for saying this - before the corpses of our valiant dead knights begin to corrupt. If there be someone skilled in the arts of medicine who will help us, these poor bodies should be examined; they may tell us enough so we can discern the cause of their deaths. And there may also be other signs to be found that will lead us closer to unravelling these mysteries."

Vincent seized immediately on this, saying "Brave Stephen, you speak good sense; there is an old teacher of mine who is adept in alchemy, physic and divination. He must accompany you to the scene, if he is willing, but since speed is of the essence here, we will have to discover a way of travelling that will get you there with the least delay."

Kit leapt to his feet "I have been a horse and an owl and a mouse before. And our Belinda too has transformed many times into different forms. We could each of us become winged horses; I could carry Captain Stephen as I have before, and Belinda the physician. What think you of this?"

Musgrave then rose, and with a sweep of her hand, commanded everyone's attention.

"I heartily concur with Captain Stephen's plan, and also with the boy's suggestion; but I would like to add to them. We all know that matters are urgent, so we should miss no opportunities. Yes, Arbutius the sage should go, and Stephen of course, but there is another whose experience and knowledge of the enemy should not be overlooked."

"I speak of myself – I will eagerly join the party! Either Belinda or Kit will surely be able, as a winged steed, to carry both me and Arbutius - why, that ancient wizened soul can hardly weigh more than a kitten!"

And then Osric spoke up, looking anxious, "But who will tend to the King's injuries, if Arbutius goes to the glade?" Vincent reassured him, saying, "We know the King has broken his legs -

we have nurses here who are used to splints and bandages. I myself had a broken wrist strapped by them not a twelve-month since, which healed swiftly. And, lest you forget, I myself am adept in many of the arcane arts!"

Within an hour, all was ready. Arbutius was found in his attic in the castle keep - he complained, out of form, but he was obviously as keen to go as his companions. He carried with him an ancient satchel (which he always claimed was made of dragon leather), which he slung over his back, saying "I will need both my hands to cling on with - I have no wish to plunge to earth mid-journey!"

And then they were on their way, following the road towards the woods. Not twenty minutes had passed, Stephen thought, when they saw, far below (for they were flying high so as not to draw too much attention), the straggling troupe of horses and men, with the horse-litter carrying the King. Stephen guessed that they would take no more than an hour or two to reach the castle.

And then they could see the Bluebell Wood ahead, and the two flying steeds swooped down to follow the track. They traced it, until Belinda recognized the site of the ambush, and then alighted, the riders dismounted, and Belinda and Kit resumed human form.

Chapter Twelve

They had all set down in the glade where Belinda had waited that day; without delay she started to lead the others down the road towards the scene of the attack.

"We shall see the graves of the noble knights soon," she said, "Each is marked by his sword, thrust into the ground, with his helm on top; the swords are serving as crosses, for want of anything more seemly; later they will all be given a decent Christian burial."

And indeed, they espied the first of them through the trees, for they had been set a few yards aside from the road. But as they drew near, they drew astonished breaths and exclaimed at what they saw. The swords and helms were there, right enough, but each was now at the head of a dark pool of water, the length of a man's height, and surrounded by feathery rushes, with water lilies floating. Eight grave-pools they counted, and pious little Belinda fell to her knees and prayed.

Stephen was the first to gather his wits and speak "Tell us, Belinda, how did this place look when you and the company started back home? Not as we see it now, I'll warrant?"

"No, no, Captain. The graves were but scrapes, covered roughly with branches and sods. The rest of the troop had only the use of a mattock and an axe carried by one of the pack-horses, which were sometimes needed for making camp on a longish journey, so they said."

Musgrave had been casting about, in and out of the trees, trying to see if there was anything further to be found, and they heard her call out again in surprise, "Here, here, come and see what more our adversary has left us!"

She was bending over a pale patch on the hard surface of the road, and peering at some markings there. "Look closely at what we have here - can it be writing? It is neither English nor Latin, for I can read both of those. Sage Arbutius, what say you?"

The aged physician hastened to join her, and, putting down his satchel, took out from it a battered pair of spectacles, bound together with string at the nose-piece. He crouched down and squinted at the markings. "Ah ha! Tis well you brought me along this day, for I am one of the few scholars in this land who can tell what this is and what it says: it is written in the runic script that the Norsemen brought with them. But, my Lady Musgrave, you were not quite right, it is indeed in Latin - it was the letters that deceived you."

"Can you tell us what it says, then?" Thus spoke up Kit, who had been silent so far, but had been surveying the grave-pools with Stephen, looking for whatever they could find that might be helpful evidence for unravelling the mystery they were faced with.

"Aye, that I can, my young friend, but it will take me a while to puzzle out, and I must copy these words onto parchment first, else they will be gone the first time it rains." He dived again into his dragon-skin satchel, and drew out a bundle of parchment. Kit could see that some sheets had been used and reused, with lines of writing criss-crossing one another. Arbutius shuffled through until he found a page that had only been used on one side, delved again for a quill and ink-horn, and started to transcribe the words on the road. "Watch me not so closely, young Kit, or ye will make me blot this!" he said, and waved Kit away.

Kit joined Stephen and Musgrave, who had gone back to look at one of the grave-pools. Musgrave crossed herself and then bent to tug at a tussock of grass growing at its edge. "Forgive me, Sir Knight, if I disturb you," she said, and then, to Stephen, "It is as I guessed. Nothing growing here has been disturbed by human hand - this work is not by mortal men!" She pulled up her long sleeve and plunged her hand deep into the pool. "If we did not know otherwise, we should think this pool had been here for years," she said, and rose somewhat stiffly to her feet.

"We will have no need to rebury these poor souls," she said firmly, "to my belief they no longer rest here below. We will leave the swords and helms, too, for nobody in these parts would disturb what has all the appearance of a cemetery. Let us search some more, who knows what else we shall discover here."

But nothing further was found, and since Arbutius had finished copying, they decided to return home. Musgrave and Stephen turned their backs while Kit and Belinda became winged horses once more; Arbutius was lost in thought, no doubt beginning to puzzle out what he had just read. The three remounted and were soon on their way back to the castle.

Chapter Thirteen

When the party reached the castle, and alighted on the top terrace of the grounds, they were greeted by Vincent and a throng of others, notable among them the King's knights, standing together. All were eager to hear what the travellers would tell, and could not forbear from calling out their questions, "What found you there?", "Did you see the rats?", "Were you attacked?", "Were the graves despoiled?"

The eager hubbub of questions was halted by the Beeman, who embraced Musgrave, and Kit, his favourite, and shook the hands of the others warmly.

"The King is returned safely," he announced, "he is resting in his bedchamber, but has said he will speak with you all this evening at dinner. He has his legs strapped and splinted, but is determined not to let a small matter like two broken legs interfere with his business. Her Majesty, the Queen, has returned home and taken charge of his care, and the salve that I showed her how to prepare is working well."

"But what have you to tell us now; you can reserve the full details for the King and the assembled company later, but I, for one, am anxious to hear what it was that you found in the bluebell wood."

One by one, Stephen, Musgrave and Kit related their versions of the events in the wood, answering many questions and correcting each other on the details. Belinda did not speak, but nodded and smiled at each speech. One man, remembering about the river of rats she had described, asked her directly, "Miss Belinda, did you see the rats again?" She shook her head, but said nothing.

Finally Arbutius produced his parchment, and in a dramatic voice, with grand gestures, told what it contained.

"It is fortunate that I have studied, not only Latin, which is the language of all serious scholars, but also the Norse runes. These characters have a peculiar form, with upright strokes and small slanting branches, so they look like twigs. This is because the Norsemen were used to inscribing them on wooden boards, where the grain of the wood interferes with the marks. But you are not interested in how they are written, but in what was written."

There were a few murmurs of assent; some of his audience had begun to roll their eyes when they thought they were in for a lecture.

"So, what we have here is something of a poem, or even a riddle. I will not translate it word for word, but it goes something along these lines:

When the forests crowd in and the deer run away,
Then all men will know that a sign has been given.
When the children are taken, they'll be kept for a month,
But their hair will not grow; they'll not hunger nor thirst.
Do not strike out blindly; try to act kindly,
Look after your mother, your sister, your brother.
If the dark ones assail thee, do not be too anguished,
Let your patience prevail and we shall overcome."

Everyone in the crowd started talking together, asking one another what they understood of the writing. One woman, who had told before of finding a kitten exchanged for her baby, called out, in hope still tinged with worry, "Does this mean that my child will be given back to me? - oh say that this is so!"

Then one of the knights finally spoke up, "And what of our departed companions - you say they are no longer in the graves we dug for them - does this mean that they also will be returned?"

To these appeals, Arbutius replied, "I cannot say how we must take the meaning of this riddle, but I believe it has been given to us for a purpose - for the moment all we can do is heed its counsel of patience."

Stephen went to his room and lay down on his bed to ponder all that had happened, but then, almost at once as he thought, felt his shoulder shaken by the serving maid. "It's time to rouse yourself, Captain," she said, "they are all gathering in the dining-hall, awaiting the King."

In the hall, they were all standing about expectantly. Only Musgrave was seated at the high table, on a dais at the head of the room. And then the double doors were flung open, and the chamberlain entered and rapped thrice on the floor with his staff,

45

"His Majesty King Arnold! All rise!" Everyone was already standing, except Musgrave; she stood and made her way down the steps to the body of the hall, as the King was borne in by four servants, carrying him on a throne, with his bandaged legs supported on an extension, Queen Tabitha walking by his side. He was taken and set down, next to the Queen's throne, in a space between two tables in front of the dais. A cheer arose from the assembly, which the King acknowledged by an inclination of his head.

"Please be seated," he said. "we will start by eating and drinking, and then the speeches will begin!"

In deference to the King, the high table was left unoccupied, and Vincent, Osric and Musgrave seated themselves on the tables on each side of the thrones. Vincent beckoned Stephen, Arbutius, Kit and Belinda to sit alongside of them. A line of servants entered from the sides of the hall, bringing jugs of beer and wine, platters of roast meats and poultry of all kinds, and baskets of bread and rolls.

Chapter Fourteen

Everyone ate, drank, and talked with their neighbours, but their talk was not of the feast, good as it was, but was full of the mysteries that they could not set aside. Stephen looked around the hall, trying to get a picture of those who were present. As well as the King's own knights, all sitting together, quaffing ale and becoming progressively rather boisterous (but without overdoing it, because there still lingered a sense of foreboding), there were other soldiers. Stephen recognized the Sergeant and some of the patrol who had unwittingly escorted Kit and himself to the town. There was also a group of the Queen's ladies-in-waiting, as Stephen guessed, since one or another from time to time would go up to the Queen, curtseying and chatting, or offering her a choice fruit or filling her glass.

And there was a group of burghers gathered around the mayor of the town, distinguished by his chain of office, as well as many others, men and women, dressed neatly but plainly; Stephen took them for ordinary townsfolk and thought that King Arnold must indeed be a man who respected the humble folk as well as the nobles, as he had been assured more than once since he arrived in the town.

After an hour during which the buzz of conversation, between neighbours and across the tables, rose to an excited pitch, the Chamberlain, who had been standing behind the King and Queen, rapped again three times on the floor with his staff; "Pray silence for his Majesty, King Arnold!"

The King first apologized for not standing, and then suggested that those who could not see him well should take a place behind others who were sitting closer to him. He spoke clearly but not loudly, but the silence in his audience was such that no-one had to strain to hear him (save for Arbutius, who held his hand dramatically behind his ear; Stephen thought privately that this was another of the old man's conceits — the sage had never shown any signs of being hard of hearing before).

"I shall start by saying how grateful I am to my faithful Knights, who stood by me when we were assailed. And I must also thank Master Arbutius, Lady Musgrave, Captain Stephen and my dear young friends Kit and Belinda for venturing out to see what they

47

could discover at the bluebell wood. Altogether, Vincent, Osric and these five have been able to gather together a valuable body of facts, and reasoned conjectures, that will help us in untangling this web of strange and frightening happenings which culminated in the glade; was it only yesterday?"

He then recounted the events as he understood them. All had heard one version or another before, but, as Stephen thought, this discourse was still a worthwhile undertaking and would ensure that all who wished to contribute to the discussion would start from a common base. When the King had finished, he invited those who wished to speak to signal that willingness, commanding the Chamberlain to call on them in turn, an orderly manner, so that a rowdy hubbub would not develop.

One of the first to rise was a knight, not tall, but of a sturdy build. Today he was wearing a padded jerkin over a white linen shirt, but still with plain hose and riding boots. "Your Majesties and all here present, you will know that I am Theobald of the Spinney. I have but two things to say. First, to give thanks for my life and that of my companions. Second to confess that I have only just recalled picking up something in those woods, as I recovered from the affray, which I thrust into my pouch at the time and have forgotten till now; here it is!"

He held up something small, and as those close enough made out what it was, there were gasps and cries of revulsion; it appeared to be a rat or some other creature. He went on, "Young Belinda spoke of a river of rats, did she not? Well this may well be one of that company!"

At this, Arbutius made his way to the knight, saying, "Sir Theobald, may I examine your trophy? I have made a study of creatures of the wild, and might be able to divine whether or no this be a common rat, or perhaps some creature more exotic."

He took it rather gingerly, expecting it to be somewhat decayed, and brought it close to his face to inspect it; but then astonished everyone in the hall by bursting into laughter that stopped him speaking for a while. When he had recovered, and dried his eyes on his sleeve, he addressed the knight, "Are you sure, sir, that you have had this with you ever since you picked it up in the wood?" Theobald, rather truculently, insisted that he had, "Why do you ask that?" he said.

"Why, because this is not a creature at all, but a toy! This is the work of an expert seamstress and embroiderer — it is sewn from fine silks and velvets, with such stitches that are so tiny as to be hardly visible; and it is stuffed, by the feel of it, with sawdust!"

Consternation was general through the hall; those close to Arbutius craned forward to get a better look at the object. Stephen noticed that Vincent had moved close to the King and was talking to him earnestly; he soon ended the conversation, and bowing to King Arnold, held up his hands in an appeal for silence.

"Friends" he said, "we must take this seriously. Let me ask our little lady Belinda to tell us more of what she saw that fateful day in the glade. Belinda, my child, you are the only one who saw what you called at the time a river of rats, can it be that they were not living creatures but toys like this?"

Belinda was not at all disconcerted by this question. She thought for a moment, evidently trying to recall what she had seen, and then spoke up clearly, "Sir Vincent and your Majesty, and all here, I can tell you that there were so many of what I called rats that it was not possible to say what each of them was like. But if they were indeed toys like this one, how could they scuttle along in such a teeming throng that day? They were pouring along the track, indeed very like a river."

Vincent reassured her that no-one was blaming her for such a mistake; "we cannot tell whether or not those you saw were like this little doll. What I begin to think is that, whatever we are dealing with, we see mainly the tricks of an illusionist, rather than those of a true magician. At the Whitsuntide fair last year there was a man who played with a white mouse on his hands — it ran across them and jumped from one to the other, as lively as you please. But when I looked closely, I saw that it was made out of candle-wax and was tied to his shirt with a fine black thread, so that really it was only his hands that moved under the so-called mouse."

"We have heard account of many strange happenings over the last few months, but which of them caused any serious harm?" Turning to the King, he said "Forgive me, sire, I do not wish to belittle your injuries — two broken legs are two broken legs — but what caused them, in truth? Your horse threw you in the melee in the woods, and broke your Majesty's legs as he fell across them."

"We have heard many tales of missing people: Stephen's dear wife and children, several people from the town and around, and the brave Knights we took for dead — but all we know for sure is that they are missing. Otherwise there were cases of strange behaviour of animals, and meats and wines turned into stone or smoke, but none of these were a true danger to us."

Chapter Fifteen

As Vincent finished speaking, the Chamberlain once again gave three loud thumps on the floor with his staff of office, and as the buzz of conversation died, spoke out, "Pray silence for her Majesty, Queen Tabitha!"

The Queen moved to the side of her husband's throne, and stood with one hand on his shoulder.

"Your Majesty, my lords, ladies and gentlemen, I would like to add my humble contribution to all that has been said."

Stephen was surprised to hear that she spoke with an accent that was neither local nor like any other that he had heard in England. He could not yet be sure, but thought that it might have echoes of the tongues he had heard in seaports along the European coast. While he pondered, the Queen addressed Arbutius, who was still holding the rat replica.

"Please bring me that trinket, my dear teacher. You say it is the work of an embroiderer or seamstress and I know something of those arts. I may be able to discover something of its origin if I examine the work."

As she took the rat and began to study it, Stephen decided that, indeed, the Queen spoke much in the way of the people of the Low Countries; he had had many dealings with ship-masters from Rotterdam and merchants from Antwerp, and he respected them and their countrymen. The Queen spoke again.

"This object is indeed a fine piece of needlework. I and all the ladies of the court have all learned the skills of the craft, but I hazard that neither I nor any of them could do as finely as this. And the stitchwork is not English, neither is it Dutch nor Norman. I believe that this work could only have been done in Denmark, or perhaps in Norway."

"What of it? you may ask. Well, think on this; we can rule out of contention thoughts we may have had about any local origin of this toy. And if the toy be from those northern lands, why then, so might be the other actors in this play — they are certainly foreign to these parts."

The King clasped her hand, "Thank you, my beloved, thou hast started a train of thought in my befuddled head. Think you, perchance, that we may be dealing with some person or persons from one of those Viking townships that still persist along our eastern coast? There are some who claim that we saw the last of the invaders more than a hundred years since, but I heard tales from my men, as we camped at nights on our way to Jerusalem, of hamlets and villages where the old folk still dressed in the style of the northmen."

Arbutius had been giving signs of his impatience to speak, and now he sprang up and almost shouted, "Yes, yes, your Majesties both, did I not say that the inscription in the wood was written in the Norse fashion? We here, near the south coast, have no cause to deal with those in East Anglia, as they call it, because much of the trade starts and finishes at the port of London. Perhaps our Captain Stephen has sailed that coast in his time?"

Stephen rose to his feet. "Aye, I have indeed; I make my home in Harwich, and dock my ship there (or did once), and I used to make regular passage to Yarmouth and as far north as Grimsby — which indeed has a Viking name, they tell me, and was founded by them. I used sometimes to drink at a tavern there, and on the walls were trophies of war, including Vikings' horned helms. But I never heard anything spoken but English by the inhabitants (but 'tis a strange English up there), though the seafarers of course shared many tongues."

The King raised his hand and spoke again, "Now I shall propose our two next ventures: first we must provide Captain Stephen with a ship — bought, borrowed or commandeered — and his choice of stout crew, so that he may sail the coast and discover whether there are indeed any of these Viking settlements left, which are more than villages full of old folk gossiping about brave times gone by. And while he pursues those enquiries, we must do the same, but locally, to find men or women with connections to the Norsemen, who may have reasons to frighten us all, or worse, to do us actual harm."

"Stephen, Vincent, Musgrave, Osric — do you agree — is this enterprise worthwhile?"

Chapter Sixteen

Stephen looked at Vincent, and happily nodded his agreement, while Musgrave, Osric and young Kit moved to join him, grasping his hands and slapping his back in congratulation. His decision being thus assented to, the King addressed the throng once more.

"Oh, my people, I am suddenly greatly encouraged; I now feel that we are about to take some purposeful action, when up to now we have been but casting about aimlessly. A few of us will now withdraw and start drawing up our plan of campaign. I invite everyone else to remain in this hall for the rest of the evening and relax and enjoy themselves. If anyone should think, now or later, of some scheme that might be added to our grand plan, then he or she should put it to my Chamberlain or to any of Vincent's company."

Over the next two days there was much discussion of ways and means. Kit and Belinda, and another child, Anthony, who could also change shape, were dispatched, in the form of pigeons, to the nearest seaport, Hastings, at Stephen's suggestion, to make enquiries about a ship and seafaring men who might be willing to sign up. Kit carried with him a warrant from King Arnold that would serve to convince ship-owners that the enterprise was a serious one. The final selection of both ship and crew would have to be left to Stephen, of course, but Kit and the others were given intense lessons on ships and the sea, so they would have some notion of what they were looking for.

Musgrave had again insisted that she was an essential member of the expedition; Vincent would also accompany Stephen, but old Arbutius was told that he would be more valuable if he stayed at the castle. He tried to protest, insisting that his knowledge of the Runic script would be necessary, but Vincent gently pointed out that they would be looking for folk who, though they might be of Viking descent, must have been living in England for some time and would understand the language. And three of the King's knights, Sir Theobald of the Spinney, Sir Maximilian the Cornishman and Sir Desmond Wilbraham, were to come with the party, since none could say whether or not any resistance would be met.

Plans were made for the journey; having travelled with the party to Hastings by horse and by coach, Stephen would inspect the ships found by the young messengers and select one for the passage to Harwich. During that voyage he would judge her suitability for the main venture, and if needs be would try again in Harwich. Each of the knights took charge of an ample purse of gold for the purchase.

Then they would set sail from Hastings, with a skeleton crew if necessary, and make their way to Harwich, Stephen's home port. He was confident that there he could assemble a crew of sailors that he already knew — he had been quartered in that town for long enough that he knew many of the seamen who frequented the port; the custom in those days was that, apart from key members like the steersman and supercargo, most men signed up anew for each voyage.

On the morning of the third day, two pigeons flew back to the castle and regained the forms of Belinda and Anthony. "Where is Kit? Is he safe?" cried Stephen.

"He is indeed safe," replied Belinda, and then burst into tears. It was some minutes before she was able to compose herself enough to explain. "He is still in Hastings, in the house of a good woman, but ..." and she wept again, " ... but he has lost the power to change his shape. When we were to fly back, he found that the power had left him!"

Vincent nodded gravely, "Aye, I was expecting this. The lad could not stay a boy for ever. But what he does not know, because I have kept it to myself, is that he will find that he has other magical powers that will stand him in good stead. I will instruct him of these when next we meet."

Amidst acclamation from all, Stephen, Vincent and their companions set off from the green in front of the castle, but taking this time, not the fateful road to the bluebell wood, but the road that Stephen and Kit had arrived by; it seemed so long ago, but Stephen realized it was not yet a week.

Chapter Seventeen

The company set off, with first a four-horse coach, with Vincent, Lady Musgrave, Stephen and Belinda riding inside, and Anthony, the third of the shape-changing children that Stephen had met, up front with the driver, a regular coachman from the castle, called Weasel (for some reason that Stephen was not told - when he asked anyone, they would grin and change the subject). Then there was a wagon drawn by two horses, for supplies and equipment, driven by a groom from the castle stables, and four riders, the three knights and the King's chief guard, Erik, tall and red-bearded, who claimed Viking ancestry.

Before an hour had passed, they came upon old Rollo, the King's road-mender, with two hefty helpers, repairing the road where the stream had broken across it. There was much hearty jesting as news was exchanged and the coachman jeered (but cheerfully) at the quality of the road work. Fortunately, enough of the repairs had been done that, once all the passengers had got out of the coach, it could be slowly manoeuvred on to the good part of the road. The wagon needed help from the shoulders of the roadmen and two of the knights, but it, too, was soon back in action.

There were no further delays and, after passing through several villages where the locals lined the roadside, cheering, there was a glimpse of sea ahead as they crested the downs and descended into the outskirts of Hastings, a town that Stephen judged was of a size with Woodhampton. He had docked there several times in the past, but had never needed to visit the main parts of the town. As it was now getting toward dusk, they conferred and decided to seek shelter for the night, so they would be fit to inspect ships the next morning.

Having found an inn not far from the harbour, that Stephen had recalled from a previous visit, Belinda and Anthony, a plump, black-haired, cheerful boy, a little younger than Belinda, were dispatched to find Kit and bring him to join the rest of the group. Meanwhile the horses were stabled in the inn yard, and the coach and wagon were left there too, guarded by two huge black dogs that Vincent had somehow found; Stephen wondered whether they were natural or had been conjured up by Vincent, but he decided not to ask yet.

While everyone of the expedition was settling down at one end of the main barn-like room of the inn, resting their bones after the ride (for even the coach was not luxurious, having no springs to speak of), and quenching their thirst with ale, the children skipped in. Belinda excitedly led Kit to where Vincent and Stephen were sitting, saying "Speak up, Kit, tell them what we found yesterday!"

Kit appeared to be in a grave mood, both due to the importance of the occasion and also, Stephen guessed, because he was still coming to terms with his loss of transformation powers. Vincent must have sensed this too, because he gathered the boy in his arms and praised him heartily; then "Come here, everyone!" he called "and Master Kit will tell us what he has discovered, and what our next steps will be!"

Kit seemed to brighten, but started by making reservations, "I know not whether what we found will be of best service to our cause, but at least we found that there are ships to be had here and now. From what little I learnt of ships before we set out for Hastings, I would say there are two that might suit Captain Stephen, and he is the only one who can properly judge them. There is first a single masted vessel which its owner called a cog. It is square-rigged, steered by an old-fashioned side oar and would need, he said, a master familiar with that way of steering, and a crew of at least twelve men, though it would ordinarily need more if it were carrying cargo. The second we saw is a two-masted caravelle, the main-mast square-rigged and the other carrying a lateen sail. It has a stern rudder, is steered with a wheel, and would need a crew of twenty, so its owner said. He is a merchant of this town, and not a seafarer himself. His captain and crew have refused to sail his ship any more, because they claim he cheated them of their proper wages; I do not know if that is true. I believe that if Captain Stephen were to choose this vessel, he would get it at a good price on that account."

Stephen thanked Kit and proposed that the next day, after breaking their fast, he and Kit and Vincent, and at least one of the knights, should inspect these ships and conclude a bargain if possible. There was general assent, and everyone prepared to have a meal and relax. But then Vincent stood up and said "Before we disperse, there is a serious matter to conclude between me and my faithful Kit. All must hear this, as you will understand as I go on. Come here, my lad."

56

Kit came forward and knelt before his master. Vincent put his hands on the boy's shoulders and spoke softly but clearly.

"You have been deeply disappointed in the loss of your transforming powers, even though you have understood for some time that this was bound to happen. But what I have to say now may be of some consolation, because I shall tell you of three new powers which you will carry for the rest of your days, and which may well be of even greater service, to you and to others, than those you have lost. Give me your hands."

Vincent took Kit's hands between his palms and went on.

"The first of these powers you will not often have occasion to call upon; but when you do it will be invaluable. This is the gift of tongues; from now and henceforth, you will be able to understand and speak in any language spoken on earth. Listen!"

Vincent started declaiming in what Stephen recognized was old Norman French, that he had heard often, while only picking up a word here or there, and then Kit, haltingly at first, but then with growing confidence, replied at length in the same tongue, with an increasingly happy expression on his face. Vincent, too, smiled happily and then continued.

"The second and third powers are related; they are the gifts of veracity. If, Kit, you look anyone in the eyes, he or she will be compelled to tell you the truth. And, by the same token, they will believe what you tell them without question. Of course, you will be incapable of speaking anything but the truth yourself; this is payment for the gifts! So, Kit, what do you say?"

Kit's only reply was to hug Vincent warmly, with tears streaming down his face.

Chapter Eighteen

The next morning, after a fine breakfast of eggs and ham, Stephen, Kit, Vincent and Sir Maximilian the Cornishman, with Belinda and Anthony in train, not wanting to miss anything, set out for the docks. Kit led the way to the first ship he had described, which appeared now to be readying for sea. Seamen and dock labourers were carrying sacks and casks aboard over planks balanced precariously on the dock and the ship's side, and stowing them in rows along the bottom of the hull. There were no decks, except for a forecastle ahead of the single mast. Standing on this and overseeing the activity was a tall bearded man.

Taking him for the master of the vessel, Stephen hallooed him, "Will you catch the tide, friend? If you are up and away, then it is little use asking if your ship may be bought or hired." The master laughed and agreed, "If you had come two days ago, I might have bargained with you — I am always ready to consider offers — but yesterday I contracted to run this cargo across to Holland, and I might well pick up further commissions there. If I am not so lucky, I will be back in three or four days and will gladly talk with you then."

Stephen waved his thanks and wished him safe passage. Turning to the others he said, more quietly, "I am not too disappointed — I know these cogs; they are skittish in any sort of running sea, and being square rigged, difficult to make way against an unfavourable wind, Besides, I have come to be accustomed to a vessel with decks and a proper hold for goods. Lead on, Kit and show us the other ship you picked out for us."

The docks, starting off as well-built stone structures at the head of the harbour, became hardly more than banks of sand and rocks the further as they extended away from the open sea. As the band picked their way along, Stephen explained that, like many a port along the south and east coasts, this one was continually under the onslaught of the sea. Some, like here at Hastings, were in danger of silting up, while in other places the action of the tides had taken whole villages away.

Soon they saw a neat little two-masted ship, at anchor a cable's length from the dock, evidently not manned. Sitting on a box on the dock, apparently keeping guard, was an old, weather-beaten man; Stephen addressed him, "Good morning to ye, grandpa, do you know where we might find the master of this vessel?" "Why sir, you'll not find the master, nor yet any of the crew; they all be gone — some to sign on with a ship that's sailing today — you might have seen it as you came along. Others have left the sea for now and gone back to their homes, sickened with being cheated. The owner, now, I can tell you where you might find him — drinking away his troubles likely — in that inn yonder." He indicated a tumbledown shack across from the dock, one of a row of similar dubious-looking buildings. "The ship is named Mary Elizabeth, anyone will point out her owner to you."

The inn, as the group ventured into it with some apprehension, not knowing what to expect, held no more than a handful of rough-looking men, mostly sprawled out on the rush-strewn floor, seemingly sleeping off a night of carousing. Two of them were still awake, seated at a rough-hewn table, playing a game of cards, with a pile of silver coins and a wicked-looking dagger before each of them.

Stephen addressed them with some trepidation, thinking that neither of them was one he would trust for a moment. "Good morrow, sirs, where would I find the owner of the Mary Elizabeth, as I would deal with him?" The stouter of the two, whose clothes, though now filthy with grease, seemed once to have been of some quality, grunted in reply, "That is I, what business do you have with me?" His companion, annoyed at the interruption, swept the cards onto the floor, picked up his pile of coins and his weapon, and staggered away to join the sleepers in a corner.

Stephen went on, "They tell me that you have had disputes with your ship's master and his crew; that is none of my business, but it makes me think that you might not refuse an opportunity to be rid of the ship and of all the difficulties she has brought you." The ship-owner wiped his forehead with a dirty kerchief and beckoned Stephen to sit opposite him. "Well, I might be persuaded to part with her" he replied, "but I doubt a man like you could afford her price; she is a fine vessel and I will have no difficulty finding a new master and crew, for I'm known around these parts as a wealthy merchant with much fine cargo to move. However, name a price, and we can start to deal, perhaps."

Stephen called Kit over, saying to the merchant, "My prentice, here, needs to learn about business; when he is grown he will be my agent. If you have no objection he will listen while we bargain."

Then with no further ado, Kit asked the man outright, looking into his eyes "Yes, sir, my captain would know what you would call a fair price. What is the least that you would take for the vessel?"

The merchant, with a somewhat puzzled expression on his face, immediately named a sum of guineas; Kit nodded and Stephen called Sir Maximilian over, who took out a pouch and poured gold coins onto the table to the amount named. "Is it a bargain, then?" said Stephen, and the merchant, still bemused at himself, nodded his assent and gathered up the coins.

Chapter Nineteen

The merchant rose from the table, with nothing but a curt further nod to Stephen, and, going to a door at the back of the room, rapped on it and called out "Where are you, inn-keeper? I need some more wine!"

After a few moments, a man in disheveled clothes appeared, rubbing his eyes. He went to a chest and produced a flagon of wine that he gave to the man, who snatched it and immediately raised it to his lips.

The landlord, seeing Stephen, Kit and the others, said affably to them, "Now gentlemen, can I get you anything? Food, perhaps, or beer or wine?"

Vincent stepped forward and answered him, saying, "Not at this hour, we think! But tell me, where would be the best place round here to look for seamen to crew our new vessel, that our friend here has just generously sold us?" The merchant scowled at this, but simply walked away without offering any comment and went to sit with his former card partner.

The landlord called out, through the back door, "Jack, you lazy lad, where are you, I have a job for you." In a moment, a boy of about Kit's age appeared, yawning and, like the inn-keeper, rubbing his eyes. "Take these gentlemen down to Widow Forester's rooming house, and look alive now!" Turning back to Vincent and Stephen, he went on, "Some of the crew from the Mary Elizabeth lodge there — they are avoiding my house while their former owner bides here! And they will know where else their former shipmates can be found, I should think."

The inn-keeper's boy led Stephen and his companions through a maze of alleys behind the inns and warehouses that lined the dock, to a big rambling house facing the main dock, in front of which was a long bench. On this were sitting half a dozen men, two of them mending a fishing net between them, others just sitting and yarning, spitting into the water and watching a fleet of two or three small fishing boats coming in to tie up.

Stephen greeted them, saying "Good morrow, mates, does anyone fancy a passage up the coast with me in my new vessel, the Mary Elizabeth? I need a steersman, a boatswain, at least half a dozen deckhands and a cook!" The idlers took notice, and rose to their feet, one saying "As long as Master Spenser is no longer the owner, I would gladly sign on again to the Mary right away! And I know that there are more of my ship-mates that feel the same. Give me your penny, and I will go and find them!" Stephen pressed a coin into his hand, establishing a traditional binding contract, and the man disappeared into the rooming-house whistling merrily.

A second man stood up and explained that he was a steersman, that he had been offered a place on the cog that had just sailed, but that he "Didn't get on with they side-oar steering fix-ups" so had declined the offer. Stephen said "If you know the Mary Elizabeth, you're the man for me, so come aboard with us!", and he gave him a penny, too.

By late morning, a crew of fifteen men had been assembled, and Stephen was telling them that they were headed East and North, around the Kentish coast and across the mouth of the Thames estuary, with Harwich as their goal. He guessed that they might make Gravesend that evening, but he would decide whether to put in there or ride out the night at anchor, depending on the breezes and how far out to sea they would have to stand so as to avoid the treacherous sandbanks of the area. Most of the crew set out to board the ship; one of their number who had been first mate on previous voyages, undertook to get them started on readying the Mary for sea.

Stephen then got a group of four fishermen to agree to row their boat to the Mary Elizabeth and prepare to tow it to the harbour mouth. "There's no chance of catching a breeze where she lies now" he explained, "but we'll walk up there first. They can row across and pull her to the wall for us all to board."

Within an hour, sails had been set, they were at the harbour entrance ready to catch a promised breeze, and Stephen was directing the crew what to do next. Kit and Vincent could see that they were experienced seamen; most of them had sailed in the Mary already, so they fell into their appointed tasks with ease. Belinda and Anthony had to be told to keep out of the men's way — neither had been on a ship before, so they were poking into everything. Sir Maximilian, Lady Musgrave and Vincent were content to take their ease resting against the forecastle rail, and Kit was already acting as though he were first mate, under Stephen's benevolent but somewhat amused gaze.

Red-bearded Erik was pacing the deck, as though anxious for action. The other two knights had agreed to take charge of the coachman with the coach, the cart and driver and the horses and take them back to the castle, vouchsafing that they had had enough of sea travel on their way off to the Crusades and did not wish ever to be sea-sick like that again!

Soon they were under way, all sails filled, and making good headway while still within sight of the coast. Stephen called the two children to him, "Soon, my dears, I will have an important task for you. Can you take on the form of seagulls? — No, not now! — I don't want the crew alarmed; they are not used to such marvels. When you do change, you must do it as privately as possible. I need some further explanation, too. If you have the form of a particular creature, do you also have all its talents? For example, I have seen sea-gulls patrolling the skies who suddenly spot a fat fish and plunge into the waves to seize it. Does this mean that they can also see shoals and sandbanks invisible from a ship?"

Belinda was quick to answer, "Yes, so I believe, though I have never yet tried this myself. I suppose, from your question, that we shall be called upon to help the ship avoid such hazards, is that so? All we can do is to try and see whether we can; would you like us to make an experiment now?" Stephen shook his head, "Not yet, but as you have guessed, we shall later today be sailing off a region where there are many shifting sandbanks. They cannot be seen from the ship, and I have only some very old charts that I found on board here; my own good charts were lost when ..."

He became quiet, and the children could see the distress that he had just awakened clouding his face.

Chapter Twenty

Late afternoon found the Mary Elizabeth approaching the notorious Goodwin Sands, a shifting series of submerged and semi-submerged sandbanks off the Kentish coast that were the graveyards of many ships and their crews. Stephen had deliberately steered away from them to the East, but, as he had explained to the children, it was impossible to know how near they were to the sands, and in what danger.

He called to Belinda and Anthony, "Now is the time for you to earn a couple of tasty fish each, my fine seagulls! See whether you can see if there are sandbanks beneath the waves that we are approaching too closely. And when you are high enough to see the true coast, look out for landmarks, such as church spires or the like, that I can use to check our progress. Try and transform now while no one of the crew sees you; it is of course, no matter if any of our own party catches a glimpse. And don't venture out of sight of the ship, or you will have to join your cousins and learn the life of wild seagulls!"

The two birds climbed swiftly, and Stephen soon lost sight of them. He went to the helmsman, praised him, and told him to hold his course; then he beckoned to Erik and asked him if he would stand in the forepeak and scan the waves ahead for sands, as an additional precaution. Said Erik, "Aye, Captain, I will, eagerly, I am a man of action and easily bored! Besides, I have sailed myself, a long time since, and still have a sailor's eye for the tricks of the sea."

After half an hour, the two seagulls returned and became Belinda and Anthony once more. Anthony was the first to report, "Captain Stephen, a league or so ahead, a long spit is stretching out across our course, which will need care; but it is breaking the surface, so its edges may be seen as a line of surf. Once we have rounded that, the main mass of sands will be behind us, we could see them clearly, even those that are well covered by the sea. Belinda will tell you about the coastline. But we didn't catch any fish!"

Stephen laughed, saying, "We shall have to find other ways of rewarding you, you have done well! Now, Belinda, what say you?" "We went a little to the North, Captain Stephen, and over ahead of us to the West we could see a cape or promontory, beyond which the coast swung round to due West, as far as we could judge. A few miles along the coast from the cape was a village of some size, with a windmill and a church with a tower, but no spire."

Stephen unrolled a chart on the deck in front of them, "Did it look something like this?" he asked, indicating a place on the chart, and when Belinda and Anthony nodded eagerly, said, "Ah hah! That is what is called the North Foreland, and it marks the mouth of the Thames estuary; but there it is too wide for anyone to recognize that it leads to a river. If the wind does not drop, I think we can round the Foreland and even make landfall at Herne, the village with the windmill, this evening, God willing."

It was as Stephen had hoped; as dusk was falling, they tied up to a jetty in a bay by the village of Herne, and leaving Erik and Maximilian on guard, walked along the foreshore until they came to an inn, where they arranged overnight accommodation and sat down to a modest but adequate meal of bread, cheese and ham. Kit was sent back to the ship with a bundle of food and a jug of ale for the two guards, who would sleep on board, taking turns to keep watch. As Stephen explained to the others "If these folks here knew us, there would be no risk of thievery or the like, but for now, to them we are complete strangers, and hence we are suspect. It is not unusual to encounter pirates along this coast, and the local folk need to be cautious."

Five minutes after he had left, Kit burst back into the inn, waving his arms and breathless. When he could speak, he almost babbled, "The rats, the rats, what are we to do? They are swarming onto the ship; I know not where Erik and Sir Maximilian are; come and see, come and see!"

Vincent and Stephen sprang to their feet and followed Kit as he ran out as abruptly as he had come in. By the time they had overtaken him they were at the jetty, and could see them, grey rats, running along the hawsers that tied the ship to the wharf, but only a few. Stephen seized Kit, embraced him, and tried to calm him down. "Be still, Kit, be still. There is nothing magic here, these are but the rats that you will find wherever ships bring or take away cargo. They are pests, but they are not a threat to us; they come out at night like this, that is why you have never seen them before. — And here are our guards, wondering what all the commotion is about!"

Indeed, Maximilian and Erik strode up, having been taking their ease sitting on some balks of timber on the jetty. Stephen and Vincent explained what had happened, and retrieved the food and drink meant for them, that Kit had set down in his haste.

"Come, come," said Stephen, soothing Kit, "you have had just too much excitement this last few days. What you need now is a good night's sleep. We must be up betimes on the morrow!"

Indeed, the next morning, dawn was just breaking when Stephen called his band together. The seamen had slept all over the floor of the inn, while Musgrave had been given the landlord's wife's room and bed. All the others, including the three children, had slept soundly in the hay-loft over the stables of the inn. The landlord had been apologetic, saying that he hardly ever had to accommodate such a large party. In less than an hour, they caught a breeze and started tacking across the estuary, bound for the Essex shore. Stephen and the helmsmen spent some of the time instructing Kit and the two youngsters in the arts of handling sails and wheel, pointing out that it was mainly the lateen sail on the after mast that enabled them to tack close against the wind.

They reached the other shore quite soon, and started to follow the coastline North towards Harwich, which Stephen reckoned they would reach before afternoon. The others could see that the prospect of seeing his home port was bringing him mixed feelings, of anticipation and misgivings.

Chapter Twenty-one

As they were crossing the estuary, the company had started to see more traffic. On the passage from Hastings to Herne, apart from numerous small fishing-boats, they had spied only two ships of any account, a trading vessel, much like the Mary, and a magnificent ship of the line, bristling with cannons, creaming along under full sail. Stephen thought it was probably from one of the Cinque Ports, maybe Dover or Sandwich, serving the King in return for the favours that he had granted to those towns, giving them the income from taxes and numerous legal rights.

Now they met a growing flow of ships of all description on their several voyages, bringing cargoes of silks and spices from the orient to the port of London, or taking English grain, woolens and linens to the world. Stephen realized how much he was missing that life, and yearned for the time when he could resume it; but for now, he had sterner duties.

They made good time, and had no need to avoid hazards, since this part of the coast was free of sandbanks or shoals, and after cutting across a wide bay and regaining the coast, it was shortly after noon that Stephen saw the familiar landmarks that told him they would soon be in Harwich. He had been instructing the helmsman in general terms, but now he stood close by him and his orders were very definite, as he guided him into the mouth of the wide inlet leading to the port.

Soon they could see the extensive wharves and docks along the waterfront; Harwich was an important port, and there were many vessels tied up, or coming in to dock, or setting sail on their voyages. Stephen was giving a continuous commentary, when suddenly he stopped talking for several seconds. The helmsman turned to see what was afoot, and then called out in alarm, "Help needed here! The captain is ill!"

Vincent and Musgrave both rushed on to the forecastle, and by then Stephen had slumped to the deck, pale and sweating. Musgrave put her arms round him and lifted him to a sitting position, "Bring water, quickly!" she exclaimed, and when Vincent passed her a flask, put it to Stephen's lips. He seemed to pull himself together, and opened his eyes. The colour started to return to his face.

"Are you yourself again?" asked Vincent, and Stephen nodded. "What happened?"; Stephen pointed ahead of the ship to the docks they were gliding towards. "That ship! The three-master flying a black pennant! That is my ship, the "Harwich Venturer"; I thought her lost with all hands, but there she floats!"

Addressing the helmsman again, he ordered him to dock behind the Venturer, and all the seamen of the crew scurried about their duties, reefing the sails so the Mary lost way as they approached the dock. Ropes were thrown to the dock workers, and they were soon securely tied up.

As soon as a gangway had been placed, Stephen, reinvigorated, gained the dock and ran towards the Venturer. As he approached the ship, he could make out the faces of the crew lining its rails and those still on shore, and he nearly felt faint once again, but shook it off, calling, "Mr Hobson, Sankey, Toby, Andrew — it is I, your Captain — tell me you know me!"

Those he addressed were obviously astounded, and could not immediately bring themselves to reply, but then they all started babbling at once, "Captain, do you live?", "We thought you drowned!", "Where have you been these last days?" and the like. But Stephen had more urgent matters in mind, "What of my beloved lady Amelia, what of Stephanie and Derek, my dear children?"

A tall man, with a shock of white hair, who the others assumed was Hobson, the first mate, for Stephen had mentioned him on a few occasions when he had been persuaded to talk of his lost friends, replied in a voice cracking with emotion, "They are all safe, in your cottage, dressed in mourning clothes, for, like us, they thought they had lost you!"

Chapter Twenty-two

Stephen immediately made as though to set off in haste to his home, but Vincent and Lady Musgrave, who by that time had come up, sought to dissuade him from this spontaneous, though completely understandable, action. Vincent grasped his arm and led him to sit down on some bales of wool on the wharf. "Think on this, Stephen," he said, "you, a man accustomed to action, who has seen many strange events over the past few days, were nonetheless almost overcome when you first set eyes on your vessel. I do not know your lady, but she has likely spent the time since you disappeared mourning your loss, consoling her children, and trying to make a new start to her life. If you were to burst in upon her, I imagine it might cause her great confusion; they say that no-one ever died of happiness, but do you want to risk all this?"

Then Musgrave spoke up, "Vincent is right. What if I visit your lady Amelia first? I can talk with her and discover her state of mind, and then I can break the joyful news to her gently, and prepare her to be reunited with you. You should keep yourself close by when I do this, of course; I warrant that she will be as eager to clasp you in her arms as you were just now to set off!"

All transpired according to these plans, and as soon as Stephen, Amelia and his children (who had to be fetched by a servant from an orchard nearby) were happily hugging each other, chatting together and relating their respective stories, Musgrave withdrew quietly and rejoined Vincent, Kit and the other two chidren. They now had a chance to admire Stephen's house, and look at the gardens that surrounded it; he was inclined, in his unassuming way, to refer to it as a 'cottage', but it was by no means as modest as that word suggests, but almost a small manor-house, with two stories.

They were taking their ease, sitting on the close-scythed lawn in front of the house, when Amelia emerged and, thanking them all profusely, asked the children's names, and embraced Musgrave and Vincent. "You must, of course, accept our hospitality for as long as you are here, you two and the three children. I will send Frederick, our gardener and stableman, to the dock to gather the rest of your crew and party and take them to Barnabas' inn, where the landlord, an old friend, will make them comfortable at my expense for as long as necessary. Thank you all again for returning my beloved husband to my arms!"

The next two days passed happily for all. Stephen took the opportunity to seek out all his crew from the Venturer and to engage half-a-dozen more; on that fateful earlier voyage, meant to be a short pleasure trip, he had made do with only ten or so men. Now he would need a full complement of at least twenty. He also purchased a cannon, powder and shot, to be mounted in the forepeak, in case of need on their voyage or at their destination, wherever it might be. Sir Maximilian asserted that he was as fine a gunner as could be found these days, and would "Take care of any rogues who tried anything suspicious!"

Another piece of business was negotiating with the men from the Mary Elizabeth. He talked to Vincent, Musgrave and Erik, and. after much discussion, proposed that Erik should take over as master of the Mary. As he had hinted, Erik had sea-going experience and had, before he joined the King's staff, been the master of an antiquated long-ship, a relic of Viking times and propelled by oars as well as a sail. This ship had finally broken up on rocks during a storm, fortunately with no loss of life, causing Erik to leave the sea for a while.

Stephen called the men of the Mary Elizabeth together and left Erik to decide whether he needed more hands. There was also the matter of obtaining a commission for a cargo; Stephen agreed that, if Erik needed any help with negotiating a contract, he would stand ready to assist. The ship, having been bought with the King's funds, would belong to him; ultimately Erik would have to offer his and the ship's services to His Majesty; he reckoned that King Arnold would be as reasonable with this proposition as he had always been in others.

Aside from business of that sort, there was much discussion of what should be done next, where should they sail and with what object. Vincent, Stephen, Musgrave and Maximilian each had their own notions, but there was common ground; all were agreed that the first thing to do was to sail up the coast to those regions that had once been the chosen settlements of Norsemen, the one that they all favoured as a first port of call being Grimsby.

Amelia was fascinated by the tales of magic and mystery related by the others; she had heard nothing of that nature herself, and neither had anyone in the town that they spoke to. Stephen even began to doubt whether they were journeying in the right direction, but Vincent and Musgrave pointed out that Harwich was a larger town than Woodhampton, and that this might have made it less of a target for their unknown adversaries. Vincent said that what had helped to spread the stories at home was that most people there were simple country folk, used to relating tall tales in the winter evenings, and therefore inclined to take notice of strange happenings, whereas the inhabitants of Harwich saw themselves as no-nonsense men of the world.

Belinda and Anthony became the close friends of Stephen's children, Stephanie and Derek. Kit felt himself a little old for some of their play, but was observed to join in enthusiastically in mock sword-fighting with sticks, and tried riding Derek's pony (having been a horse himself, but never a rider until then, he was pleased to see that riding came more easily to him than to Derek). Vincent had enjoined the other two not at any account to transform themselves merely for sport or to impress their new friends.

On the second evening, Stephen went down to Barnabas' inn, and gave instructions to his first mate, Hobson, to prepare the Venturer to sail the next morning.

Chapter Twenty-three

When, straight after breakfast, the travellers arrived at the dock, they found it in a confusion of activity. There was a number of waggons lined up, waiting to have their loads of hides and woollen cloth that had come overland from London loaded, along with bundles of fine timber from Poland destined for the specialist furniture-makers of the North. As well there were half a dozen chests of salt, from the salt-makers in Harwich.

Stephen, Vincent and Musgrave had decided that the voyage should appear to be a normal business venture, so that speculation about its purpose would not cause suspicions to be aroused.

Kit and the younger children were enthralled by the skill and effort of the wharf labourers as they operated the derrick, a long spar linked to the foot of the Venturer's mainmast; one team hoisting the loads from the wharf, with block and tackle led over the head of the derrick and the other pulling the spar back over the ship so the goods could be lowered into the hold. Bundles of timber and hides were lifted one at a time, while smaller loads were enclosed in cargo nets.

After loading, the passengers were shown to their quarters in the after part of the ship. If they were at sea overnight, Musgrave would take Stephen's night cabin — she had to soothe him and brush aside the fears that he recalled from the last time it was occupied by a woman — while Stephen would join Vincent, Kit and the other children in a large cabin also used as a chartroom and mess. Sir Maximilian chose to bed down on deck, having elected himself as sentinel.

There was a fair breeze springing up from the west, so it was possible for the Venturer to set sail without delay as soon as loading was complete and the main sails set. As the ship slowly left the dock, Stephen saw two huge black dogs, walking along with the ship and staring at its progress. He recalled seeing two such dogs at Hastings, guarding their coach and horses at the inn, and wondered once more whether Vincent had conjured them up; he resolved to ask him once they were fairly on their course for Yarmouth, their first port of call.

The breeze was strong but not blowing from an ideal quarter, so Stephen had to set course in a series of long tacks that took the vessel well out into the German Sea; after an hour or so on one heading, the steersman brought her back towards the coast once more. Stephen estimated that they were sailing three leagues to make every league of progress towards their goal, the port of Yarmouth, so that the passage, which might have taken four hours with a favourable wind, was going to take a full twelve, and they would likely arrive around dusk. But then the wind dropped almost to nothing, leaving the sails flapping idly.

Stephen called his passengers together and laid out the possible courses of action, or inaction, that offered. They could drift against a sea-anchor and ride until the breeze picked up, which might happen in an hour or not for some time. They could launch the ship's longboat, which was hanging from davits at the stern, and take turns to man the oars, eight rowers at a time, and tow the ship; but he warned that this would be exhausting work and might not take them as much as a league toward their destination. Since there was no real urgency, Stephen said he did not favour this. And then, not really meaning it, he said "There is, of course, magic!"

At this, Vincent and Musgrave turned toward each other and broke into smiles. "So what would you suggest?" asked Vincent, "should Belinda and Anthony transform into whales and draw us to port? Or should I conjure a favourable wind? Or, perchance, you have a notion that this entire ship can be carried to Yarmouth in a whirlwind? But, let me not play games with thee, there is a way, and both Lady Musgrave and I can command it."

The two clasped hands, and immediately the ship started to glide over the waves as though it were a duck paddling beneath the surface, but with no sign of such activity. The sails still hung empty on their yards, so Stephen ordered the deckhands, who were all gaping in amazement, to reef them, so they would not impede this silent progress. Kit, still knowledgeable about such matters, explained to Stephen that the men would soon make up their own explanation, which would seem convincing to them, just as the King's guards had done when he and Kit rode into Woodhampton town that first day.

The Harwich Venturer docked in Yarmouth while daylight was fading, so that no-one watching would have seen anything out of the ordinary. There was only salt to be unloaded here, for the local herring salteries, and this task was left to the crew, while Stephen and his passengers found an inn for a meal and accommodation.

As they walked along the quayside, Stephen once again caught sight of the two huge black dogs, following them at some distance. He would definitely tackle Vincent about them as soon as they were sat down at dinner.

Chapter Twenty-four

Yarmouth was a port that was very familiar to Stephen, so he led the way to a lodging-house that he had often used in the past. It was not an inn, so he gave the crew (and Sir Maximilian, who professed a mighty thirst) leave to patronize their favourite haunt near by, while he, Vincent and Musgrave and the youngsters dined in the lodgings. The landlady was glad to greet them, especially Lady Musgrave and Belinda, saying, "I never have any complaints by men about the victuals I serve them, but it takes a woman to really know what is quality fare!"

They were served a hearty vegetable soup, followed by a rich stew of mutton with barley and gobbets of fat in it, which Musgrave claimed "Would line our stomachs so we might go a week without eating again!"

When they were replete, they picked at sugar-plums and fresh cherries and sipped wine or ale while they discussed the day's events (in somewhat oblique terms, for they could easily be overheard). Stephen decided it was a good time to broach the topic of the black dogs.

"I have thought more than once that those two great hounds might be your familiars, Vincent; I hope that you do not take these speculations amiss. What puzzles me in particular is that I have seen them at several of our ports of call, at Hastings, Harwich and now here at Yarmouth. How is it that they make their passage, or is it that each pair is different?"

Vincent, as was his frequent habit, answered in a slightly mocking style, "Maybe, Captain Stephen, you think that I can conjure up such beasts at will, is it so? Well, I'll disclaim that particular power, though it would, I'll admit, be very useful from time to time. Nay, they are not my familiars, nor Lady Musgrave's neither. To tell the truth, I have no more notion than thee whence they come, or what is their purpose, if any there be. But, you forget already, we have in our company someone fluent in any language spoken in the world: Master Kit — he could ask them directly; didst thou not realize that dogs have their own language?"

So they resolved that, at the first opportunity, Kit would question the huge dogs. Meanwhile, it was time to turn in, for sailing and sea breezes had left all of them more than ready for a sound night's rest.

When they were wakened for breakfast it was already full day. After eating, Kit was sent to the inn to rouse the crew, but found they had forestalled him and were already busy aboard the Venturer, un-reefing the sails and rearranging the cargo to take account of the removal of the heavy chests of salt. Kit returned to the lodging house with Mr Hobson, the first mate, who wanted instructions from Stephen about the next leg of their voyage.

Stephen announced, to Hobson and the others, that he hoped to make Grimsby that day. As an old Viking town, this would be a good point of departure for their final quest, if perchance the descendants of the norsemen were, as they suspected, responsible for the mysterious happenings of the past weeks. From Yarmouth to Grimsby they would try to hug the coast, wind and tide permitting; Stephen now knew that they were not as reliant on these as he had previously thought, but his pride as a seafarer would not let him call on magic unless it were really necessary.

He explained to the others, Hobson occasionally nodding in confirmation, that the sea along this stretch of the coast had encroached on many settlements that once were fishing-ports and now were drowned, with the tops of buildings to be seen at low tide.

As they bade farewell to the lodging-house keeper, thanked her for her hospitality and started walking back to the ship, Kit suddenly raised his hand and motioned the party to stop. Ahead of them, lying together by the edge of the dock, were the two black dogs, heads raised and vigilant. Kit slowly walked towards them, and the others could hear that he was whimpering quietly. When he reached the dogs, he crouched down so that he no longer towered over them, and made low growling and whining noises, to which they both replied. After a while, he stood up, offered his hands for them to nuzzle, and returned to the group.

"I will relate what they told me once we are under way," he said, "there is much to discuss and there are still unanswered questions."

Within an hour, the Harwich Venturer was under a full set of sails and making good speed, the wind being in a more favourable quarter that on the day before. Stephen was hopeful of reaching Grimsby by the afternoon, so, leaving the helmsman to maintain their course, they all repaired to the chart-room for Kit's report, leaving Sir Maximilian on watch, looking for enemies, so he said.

"As I said before," Kit explained, "there is much that I do not understand in what the dogs told me. I could follow their talk quite well, but their way of thinking is not like ours, and they have not the words for many of our ideas. For one thing, they do not use names as we do, so they must describe people instead. Perhaps it would be best if I just tell it as they told me, and we can then try to make more sense of it later."

Vincent and Musgrave assented to this, and he began.

"They said they are the servants of a woman of high status (as they would describe a pack leader of their own kind). She has the power to send them wherever she will; they did not understand how, all they knew was that they would suddenly be in a new place. So they were here today, while yesterday they were in another big place with ships, which must have been Harwich. They have a word for ships, which they explained by indicating those we could see at the dock. They have much better words for things which ordinarily interest dogs, and I was able to understand those right away, somehow. They understand that their duty is to guard us, all of us, while they are with us; their mistress has made that clear to them, and they are faithful to her wishes and orders. When I asked more about their mistress, all they could tell me was that they thought she was from another country, not ours. She cannot talk with them as I can, but the human commands she uses with them are different from those they hear from our countrymen."

Vincent commented, "I suppose, then, that they do not know how the mistress knows where we are, so she can send them to us."

"No, nothing was said on that. Whenever I asked about something to do with knowing, or understanding, they seemed to be uncomfortable. I would say that a dog's life is lived in a simpler way than a human's, in the same way that an unlettered countryman of ours would have difficulty with complicated ideas; so dogs think on a more practical level than us."

Musgrave thanked Kit for his explanation and for the clear way he told it, then said, "Well, we know a little more, but not much. What I'm wondering about is the identity of the dogs' mistress. They think she might be a foreigner, but she is obviously one who has our well-being at heart, and so we must conclude she is not allied with the mysterious forces who have been harassing us. Who do we know of high degree who might have arcane powers? I cannot think of anyone at the moment; certainly none of the ladies of the court!"

Vincent suddenly slapped his thigh, "My lady, I think you have put your finger on something! I can speak freely in this company, though I would not were Sir Maximilian with us here. What do we know about her Majesty, Queen Tabitha? Is it possible that she could be the mysterious mistress of these good hounds?"

Chapter Twenty-five

Soon after leaving Yarmouth, the coastline, which they were still keeping in sight, swung to the West. After an hour, when Kit's report on his conversation with the dogs was over, Stephen called Belinda and Anthony to him.

"Now what do you say, my fine seagulls, to some more watching duty? We shall soon approach the Wash, and I want to avoid going into it too far."

"What is the Wash," said Belinda, giggling a little, "shall we launder our clothing there?"

"Nay, thou mischievous lass, it is not a wash-pot, but a great bay in the sea; it is very shallow and it would be as easy to run aground there as it was on the Goodwin sands the other day. Why, it is so shallow that at low tide men have wagered they could drive a coach and four from one side to the other; their fate was not always fortunate. If you two fly ahead, you will be able to see what is a prudent point to cast across its mouth to the North."

It was no more than half an hour when the two returned; Belinda, as usual spoke up first, "It was as you said, Captain, we could clearly see, by the colour of the sea-bottom, that we have little more space to run on this heading. With your approval, we would say that the Venturer should turn for the North almost immediately."

Stephen nodded and thanked her, than called to the helmsman, "Time to alter course for the North, Sankey; Mr Hobson, see about setting the sails for the new run. We should see Skegness in an hour or two. When the sails are set I want a man to go aloft and keep watch, for this coast changes by the month, and I have not sailed this way for nearly a year."

There was much activity and calling of orders as the men swarmed up the masts and yard-arms and while the boom of the lateen sail was swung from one side of the ship to the other. Soon the Venturer was heading North, and the thrumming of the sails and the chop of the waves on the bow were singing a different song from before.

Stephen joined the other members of the expedition, saying, "When I last tied up at Skegness, the inhabitants were still clearing up after some deadly storms had carried away many of the buildings close to the foreshore. This town was settled originally by the Vikings, who gave it its name, and for over four hundred years the people there have been carrying on a running and losing battle with the sea."

"Will we dock at Skegness?" asked Vincent. "Well, I would rather press on if the wind continues to be favourable. It's my aim to make Grimsby today if we can, since it is a bigger settlement, still with Viking roots, which will suit our plans better. The folk in Skegness have better things to do than answer our enquiries, which might sound foolish to them."

Not an hour later, there was a "Halloo!" from the watchman aloft, who reported that the ship was passing a town on the coast. Stephen nimbly took to the rigging and climbed until he, too, could see the town, "Aye, that's Skegness for certain - we've made good time. It looks as though they have rebuilt the jetty that had been swept away last time I passed this way."

Descending quickly, by sliding down a rope, he continued, to Vincent, Musgrave and Kit, "At this speed, if the breeze doesn't drop, we may well be closing on Grimsby before evening. Then our enquiries will begin in earnest, I'd hazard."

Stephen's guess would probably have been accurate but for what befell the Harwich Venturer next. The children, including Kit, had been set to work helping some crew members make the decks "ship-shape" at the suggestion of Musgrave, who said, "The devil finds work for idle hands to do!" They coiled ropes neatly, hauled sea-water up in a canvas bucket to wash down the scuppers, and generally made themselves useful. And in the midst of this activity, which they were quite enjoying, Anthony, normally a quiet boy, suddenly called out, "I hear church bells - how can that be in the midst of the ocean?"

Everyone hushed and listened, and indeed, faint but distinct, they could all hear the tolling of a bell. They were too far from the coast, and the wind was in the wrong direction for the sound to be coming from the land, so it was a mystery. Then Belinda, bright as ever, said, "This calls for some more bird work, but what bird is it that hears the most keenly? When I have been flying as a seagull or a pigeon, I have not felt I could hear particularly well."

Somehow, they all turned to Vincent, remembering his long experience with wild creatures of every sort.

"Why, the owl, of course," said he, "she hunts at night and can hear a mouse's whiskers trembling a mile away! But why must you become a bird, Belinda, can you not listen from our deck?"

But Belinda was quick to point out that the whole ship was alive with sound; from the singing of the wind through the rigging to the slap of the waves at the bow and the creaking of the timbers, there was no part of the ship that was not joining in the anthem, and would drown out the tolling they were seeking. "Yes, I'll go as an owl," she said, "but I will need a bird of the day with me, for the owl can be almost blinded by bright light. So, Anthony, wilt thou accompany me as a gull?"

In no time the two birds were climbing up and the watchers on deck could see that they were flying in ever-wider circles. Then they seemed to dart off ahead of the ship's course and make much tighter loops, and then sped back in a great swoop to land on the deck and become a boy and a girl once again.

Anthony it was who spoke first, "Belinda followed the sound of the bells - even I could hear them quite clearly as we got closer. And then we could see their source, and this was a sight that we could hardly believe!"

Belinda joined in, as excited as Anthony, "Captain Stephen, did you mark where we circled tightly? Please, take the Venturer closer and be prepared for a wonderful sight!"

Chapter Twenty-six

Without further ado, Stephen gave the necessary orders; most of the sails were reefed, and the ship lost way and drifted gently toward the general area where Belinda and Anthony had flown in circles.

Everyone was leaning over the rails and straining their eyes, but Kit climbed the rigging, thinking he might get a better view from aloft, and so it was he who first sang out, "I see something below the waves; I think we might ground on it if we do not strike our sails very soon."

Stephen and the crew took heed of this warning, and the Venturer slowed so that there was no longer a bow-wave, and the remaining sails hung loosely. Kit still had the best view, because those on the deck, leaning perilously far over the rails, were looking aslant into the sea, a view which was further limited by the ripples of the surface.

Stephen called to the first mate, "Mr Hobson, now is the time to lower the long-boat!" and this operation was soon in train. Two of the crew got into the boat as it swung from davits at the stern; ropes lashing it in place were loosened, and four strong crewmen lowered it to the surface of the sea.

Stephen climbed down a rope ladder and took his place on the centre thwart and he was soon joined by the two children and Kit, who had swiftly descended from the rigging and claimed the privilege by virtue of his original sighting. Two more crewmen joined them and the four took up their oars and started to paddle out.

Within a few strokes, Stephen and the others could begin to see what it was that waited for them beneath the waves; it looked like stonework — not rocks, but masonry. But their view was still not clear; Vincent, realizing this, called from the ship, "Belinda and Anthony; now might be a good time to try a new form — what do you think of becoming seals?"

Hardly had the words left his mouth when the two were slipping over the side of the long-boat, and with a stroke of their flippers and a toss of their long sleek heads were heading down to the mysterious building.

Meanwhile Stephen and his oarsmen were quartering the area; he could see enough to direct the boat around the outlines of the stonework, which stood out dark against the lighter sandy bottom some fathoms below. It seemed to be of considerable extent, maybe as much as two or three hundred yards long, and nearly as wide, but with an irregular outline.

The tolling bell was no longer to be heard. After an hour, two shining heads broke the surface by the boat, and Kit and Stephen helped the two explorers aboard as soon as they had regained human form. Belinda and Anthony were shivering, once they were no longer in their protective coats, so Stephen decided it was time to return to the Venturer. The two were eager to report, but he persuaded them to wait for a wider audience, back on board.

Of course, once she had been wrapped in a warm blanket, Belinda could no longer restrain herself, and spoke out excitedly.

"We were able to swim all around this building — it looked to me like a castle or, more likely a monastery. In some places, the sand is piled up against the walls, in others they are quite clear... " Anthony, hardly able to contain himself, interrupted her, "Tell about the window, tell about what we could see through it, do!"

Belinda went on, "Anthony is right, we did find a glass window, rather covered by green slime, but the most important thing was that we could see lights inside, flickering lights, like candles or rushlights — there are people in there!"

Chapter Twenty-seven

This statement was received by all in some astonishment, and there was a hubbub of questions and speculations, until Vincent raised his hand to command silence.

"Contain yourselves, please, everyone. Can we not let Belinda and Anthony first finish their accounts? They have given us one startling piece of information — let us see if there be more to come!"

So Belinda, as usual enjoying being the centre of attention, related her story, from time to time being confirmed or corrected by Anthony. She said once again that the building resembled a monastery, rather than a castle; she had been taken once, two or three years ago, to visit an uncle who had just become a monk, so she had retained a picture of such an establishment. But she said that there were, of course, no open courtyards or cloisters; if there were any similar features they were enclosed even more than those in a monastery on land. Musgrave chose this point to express a thought of her own, "If it truly be a monastery, then the bell we heard must have been the call to Vespers; the time, late afternoon, was right!"

But there were two features that caused some particular excitement; Belinda described seeing a wide arch, forming the mouth of what seemed a tunnel. The children had not ventured to enter it, being cautious of where it might lead; they had found this before seeing the window, so imagined it might be the lair of some giant sea creature. At this description, Vincent nodded his head vigourously, as though this sighting had confirmed an idea he had formed, saying "I venture that this is a way of entering the building; I would not be surprised if the tunnel were to lead to the bottom of a lake within a cavern, so that anyone entering might break the surface and find himself in breathable air, and thence gain the interior of the monastery."

Belinda carried on with her description; they had seen other windows, but had not tried peering into them, for as Anthony said "We knew not whether we would be welcome, even as seals!" The roof was generally flat, and in places the sand had drifted onto it, so the buildings could have easily been missed by casual passers-by. But the second feature that interested Vincent especially was that, leading away from the main building, in the direction of the shore, was a long gallery or tunnel, not as high as the rest of the structure. The children had, again, not followed it very far, not wanting to go too far from the boat and the Venturer, but Belinda said that it might very well reach as far as the shoreline.

"So," said Vincent, it seems our monks, if monks they be, have two entries, one from the sea, one from the land. This is good news — as much as I wish to meet these holy friars, I would have found it very difficult, not being a swimmer, to enter through the water gate! I would suggest, without more ado, that we ask Captain Stephen to take us to the nearest point on the coast, and we will see whether we can find the land entrance."

Stephen readily agreed, and Belinda was sent aloft, once more as a seagull, to guide the Venturer along the gallery, as they had begun to call it. As it transpired, this gallery was no more than three hundred yards long, and so Belinda returned to the ship almost at once, and Stephen called for the sails to be reefed and for a sea-anchor to be trailed to slow the ship to a walking pace.

The site of the undersea monastery, if such it truly was, lay at a distance of two or three miles from the general line of the coast, which was in the form, in that region, of very shallow and sandy beaches, with no elevated land beyond an interrupted line of low dunes. But they did not have to travel as far as the coast itself, for, close to the line of the gallery, there appeared a small island, no more than fifty or sixty yards across, surrounded by a broad stone revetment, and with a low squarish building in its centre. If they had not all been gazing over the rail into the sea, they would have spotted it earlier, despite its low profile.

And as the ship cautiously approached, under almost bare masts, they could all see, standing atop the building, a figure in monk's robes. As soon as they were within earshot, the man called out, "Pax vobiscum; our welcome to you, Lady Beatrice, Vincent, Captain Stephen and all your companions; I am the Abbot of Louth Minor, my name is Terence, and we here have been expecting you for some days!"

Chapter Twenty-eight

The abbot's greeting caused much excitement on board, and questions began to be flung at him from every quarter.

Smiling, he raised both arms above his head, saying, "Later, later, my friends! We first need to get your vessel docked and all of you welcomed into our modest home; no doubt none of you would refuse refreshments and victuals at this hour!"

At these words, a number of monks, with their cowls flung back and their sleeves looped up out of the way, emerged from the building and helped the crew of the Venturer bring her alongside and tie her up securely to the bollards along the sea-wall. Gangplanks were taken from their store, and soon everyone was ashore. Mr Hobson was at first inclined to remain aboard, but the abbot persuaded him to come ashore too, saying that the brothers were capable of managing everything to do with the ship, some having been mariners themselves, before they took their vows.

Everyone from the ship was led into the building, and, following the abbot, were conducted down several flights of stairs and into a large hall. "This is our refectory", explained the abbot, "You shall see the main monastery once we have eaten and drunk, and after I have bored you with an account of our history — this is the penance we exact from all our guests!"

Once all were seated, travellers and monks together, and were enjoying the cold meats, breads and fruit that had been set before them, and quaffing the ale that they were told was brewed within the abbey, Abbot Terence rose and everyone fell silent to hear his address.

"This abbey was established more then a hundred and seventy years ago; but not in its present form. Originally it was a monastery like many others, with gardens and farm fields all around. It was within sight of the coast, but comfortably inland from it. Starting in a small way, as a daughter establishment of the main abbey at Grimsby, it was intended to serve the communities in the farmlands in this part of the shire, and grew slowly for thirty or forty years."

"But it was to be beset by storms and high tides, which took away great swaths of the low-lying land, until the main buildings themselves were threatened. But our order has great determination, and the abbot and brothers of the time were not dismayed; with God's help, they set about strengthening the structure, and making sure that the outside walls would be able to withstand even the direct buffeting of the seas."

"Within a year or two, what they feared came to pass; at high tide, and with an on-shore wind, our monastery was indeed often assailed by the waves. The gardens and fields were easily inundated, and so the community abandoned most of them and moved their agricultural activities further inland, where they bide until today. But they persisted with strengthening works on the main buildings, even roofing over the courtyards and cloisters. Many of our brothers, expert masons and dyke-builders, came from the low countries to assist in the work, and when the sea started to steal the land from about the monastery, all was ready for it."

"I have bored you enough! You can all make guesses at what has happened since, for what you see is the outcome of our predecessors' endeavours over a hundred years; the main abbey is snug and sound beneath the sea, and here we are, connected to it by a covered way, which can be used whatever the weather or the state of the tide. In many ways we are the envy of our brothers in other monasteries, who must put up with draughty buildings and leaking roofs!"

"If any of you have questions about our community, you have only to ask me or any of the brothers; we are all of us proud (but not overweeningly, I hope) of our house and household. But next, I will have another sort of tale to relate — you must all be puzzling over how I was able to greet some of you by name, and how it was that you were all expected! Forgive me for a moment; I must rest my bones and have a bite and a sup before I continue."

The abbot took his seat, and Vincent rose, thanking him and the brothers for their welcome, and saying "Indeed, we are all waiting with bated breath for your explanation; I myself am agog to know what, if anything, you can also tell us about those strange occurrences that drove us to set out on our quest."

The abbot suddenly leapt to his feet and cried out "Oh, I have forgotten something that will astonish you; that is what happens to me when I get engrossed in my often-told tale! Brother Adrian, please go and bring our other guests; I know they have already eaten, and are rested sufficiently for a surprising encounter!"

An elderly monk scurried out of the hall, and a few minutes later, the heavy doors reopened to admit a group of men with a child or two and a woman. At this sight, Vincent and Musgrave sprang up, but not as quickly as Sir Maximilian, who rushed forward to greet and embrace a group of somewhat bewildered men; they were the knights who had vanished from the bluebell wood, his former companions.

Chapter Twenty-nine

For a few moments all the travellers were speaking at once; asking so many questions of the knights that there was soon a noisy confusion. The abbot again exerted his authority with raised arms, "People, people, we shall get nowhere like this. I suggest we all proceed patiently to the locutory, where we can hear the accounts of our dear restored friends, and where I might tell everyone of the events that have led us to this point."

Terence and Brother Adrian led the way from the refectory past a small chapel, which the abbott explained was for the use of monks and lay brothers during their working days on land, and into the gallery. This was by no means a confined tunnel, as Stephen had imagined it might be, but an arched corridor, well illuminated by oil-lamps in sconces. The company hurried along, the buzz of conversation continuing, until they reached a lobby. On one side was an arched entrance to the main church. Several of the travellers, including Belinda, took the opportunity to enter it a few steps and kneel and murmur a prayer, until the group was led into the locutory, a large room well-equipped with chairs and small tables, a parlour where the monks could engage in informal conversation, and where visitors could be entertained.

Making sure everyone was comfortably seated, the abbot introduced the other members of the knights' group — a couple who had disappeared, assumed drowned in the river, who were now looking after a baby who had been abducted from his cradle and replaced by a kitten; he also explained that, in the monastery stables, they were keeping farm animals and dogs and cats, all presumed lost by their owners.

Then he turned to the knights, "Which of you will tell us what transpired after the terrible shocks of the bluebell wood? The last that any one of our expeditioners knows is that you and your comrades were buried there in shallow graves!"

A tall knight with a yellow beard stood up, "For those as don't know me, I am Sir Edgar of Wisbech. I've told this story more'n once, so I hopes as I won't leave anything out. Well, here goes. As his reverence says, we was buried — but we knew nothing of this, thank the Lord, because we was out of it; it gives me the horrors thinking of it even now. The first we knew after that, we was lying in bed in a hospital, with the holy sisters ministering to us. They soon had us up and about, and we found out we was in the nunnery as goes with this monastery, a sister of it you might say. Only that's on dry land, a league or so away from here. Then we was brought here, and abbot Terence explained that we had to keep our heads down for a while, until proper steps could be taken. There's always them others lurkin' about, you see, and we mustn't show 'em our hands. So we was specially pleased to see Vincent, Captain Stephen and her ladyship and the others had arrived, so now we can start doing something instead of sittin' around waitin'."

The abbot took over. "Thank you, Sir Edgar, you've given us the main facts. Now I had better provide our guests with some explanations of why and how we at the abbey are involved, and what has been going on. Well, it all starts off with our devoted friend, Her Majesty, Queen Tabitha." — Vincent, Musgrave and Stephen exchanged wide-eyed looks at this — "She, as a young woman, was a postulant of this Order, and even after finding that a nun's life was not for her has kept her ties with us. Every year she comes on retreat here, the last time only a few days ago. As you know, she returned to Woodhampton Castle just after the attack in the bluebell wood, in time to tend to the King's injuries."

"While on retreat, she discussed the strange happenings that are your chief reason for your expedition, and came to the conclusion, with us, that they are being caused by a malevolent being or group, in possession of black powers. But again, as a result of these discussions, she and we decided that they were not so formidable as to be immune from right-minded retaliation. Her Majesty, like her dear associates, Vincent and Lady Beatrice, has certain arcane powers herself, and resolved to enlist them in this endeavour. But she realised, and we agreed, that great subtlety must be employed; our opponent or opponents would not refrain from unfair practices if they felt at risk of failing."

"But, you are asking, how did the knights get here from their graves, and the others, too, after their disappearance or transformation? And I know that the Queen's faithful black dogs have made you puzzle, too. Well, this all depends on the greatest magic of all, but when I tell you about it you will be more amazed by its simplicity than by its power; it all depends on dreaming — I wonder that Vincent and Lady Musgrave have not bethought themselves of it already!"

This remark caused Vincent to burst out in a roar of laughter and to slap his forehead, "Of course, of course! How easy it is to overlook something as normal and natural as that! We all do it every day, but we forget that we each have such a miraculous power. Give me the chance to explain, abbot Terence, if you would be so kind!"

Chapter Thirty

Vincent started his talk, putting his hand on the abbot's shoulder. "As you will have understood, our good abbot and his order of friars do not reject magic, but embrace it. Some other Christian orders forbid magic, saying that it is ungodly, but how can this be, seeing it is God-given? It all starts with dreams, and every human can dream. And even dumb animals can and do — who has not seen their dog, sleeping by the fire, dream about chasing rabbits? His paws and legs move in little running motions, and he whimpers softly, thinking he is barking. So, of course, dreaming is natural and universal."

The abbot smiled and nodded, and gestured his affirmation of Vincent's words to the audience; Vincent continued:

"Many of us are content to accept whatever dreams we are given, whether they are pleasant or not; we all know the distress that a nightmare can bring, and the experience of waking in fright, sweating and trembling. But a few are able to take their dreaming further; they find that, once they have realized they are dreaming, they can direct the course of their dream, doing what they yearn to do in waking life but cannot, like flying with the birds, or communing with unattainable people. This realization that dreams can be controlled also helps to take away the dread of nightmares."

"But there is a further step that dreaming can take; a step that not everyone can manage, and one that leads us to what others can only see as magic. All little babies, I believe, are born with magical abilities, but they soon lose them as they learn about the physical world in which we are all constrained to live — But now, I see that many who listen to me are starting to wander and to wonder whether they can essay these arts themselves! I will talk further on this to anyone who wishes, at a later moment. I have rudely interrupted Terence's account of the events that have brought us here; please continue, Sir Abbot."

The abbott took over, "Please do not apologize, Vincent, what you say is relevant to my story, of course. I was telling how the knights were taken from their graves and brought under our care. It was like this: as soon as Queen Tabitha had made sure that King Arnold's wounds were receiving the best attention at the castle, she dreamt herself to the Bluebell wood — I see that this simple statement is causing general awe and incredulity, have you so quickly forgotten what Vincent was telling us, and can you not believe that her Majesty could be an adept in the dreaming arts — as I say, she dreamt herself to the Bluebell wood and, leaving her message on the road, then dreamt that all the knights were in the nuns' hospital and that the graves had become pools."

"Since I see that many of you are still shaking your heads and looking doubtful, I will enlarge a little on what it is to use dreaming to have effects on the physical world. To move to a new place is the simplest outcome; while dreaming, one simply imagines travel to the new place, and then 'wakes up' there. I cannot explain it more — only those who can do it could understand — just as I cannot explain in words to a little child how to move his hand. Nevertheless, I will try to describe how our Queen did something much more difficult; how she moved the knights to a new place."

"First of all, she dreamt herself to the bluebell wood; I have said already how this is done. The next step was to join each knight in their own dream. They were not merely asleep, they were swooning under the effects of the noxious fumes with which they had been attacked, but still they were dreaming. In her own dream, she could see the knights, below ground as they were, and could simply awaken them, as one does in the ordinary world. Then, as a group, all the knights could move to the nuns' hospital, under the Queen's direction, lying down on the beds there while still dreaming. Then all that was necessary was for them to wait to wake up in the normal way — which they would have eventually done in their graves; imagine the horror of that!"

"I will not go into the other things the Queen did at that time, changing the graves to pools and writing the message; they are not important. And I will also leave you to imagine how she managed her faithful black dogs."

Vincent thanked the abbot, and addressing the audience again, said, "You may be asking yourselves: if one woman, however eminent, can do all this while dreaming, why was it necessary to arrange this expedition, recover Stephen's ship and bring so many people with us on our quest? Well the answer is simple: our opponents can dream, too, and if we were to attempt to engage with them entirely in dream territory, then who knows how it might end. We already know that they think and act in evil ways and are masters of confusion, so they would have us, who must act straightforwardly and honestly, at an immediate disadvantage."

"So, what are our plans? How shall we proceed from now on? Captain Stephen; I see no reason to abandon our journey to Grimsby, which is now very close; do you agree? We thought from the outset that our adversaries have some connection with the old Nordic culture, and we know that Grimsby was founded by the vikings. It seems to me that this is still a good enough reason to start making enquiries there. Since Queen Tabitha has involved herself earnestly with our quest, I propose to ask her to join us — by the way, I am still a little puzzled why she chose the runic script for her message to us at the bluebell wood; let me recall what she wrote:

When the forests crowd in and the deer run away,
Then all men will know that a sign has been given.
When the children are taken, they'll be kept for a month,
But their hair will not grow; they'll not hunger nor thirst.
Do not strike out blindly; try to act kindly,
Look after your mother, your sister, your brother.
If the dark ones assail thee, do not be too anguished,
Let your patience prevail and we shall overcome.

Some of this begins to make sense to us now, but I'm bound to think that Her Majesty was addressing those others as much as us. Her use of runes may be part of a stratagem — we should ask her, when and if she agrees to accompany us further. Tell me, Abbot Terence, what means do you and the Queen customarily use to converse, for example when she wishes to come here on retreat?"

"Well, Vincent, it depends very much on the urgency of the occasion; if your young friends are not weary of carrying messages as pigeons, that would be a way as quick as any. None of us at the abbey are adepts at dream travel; what of your companions, would they be able to go thus?"

Musgrave seemed about to speak, but Vincent laid his hand on her arm, saying "As I said before, we assume that our opponents can draw on their resources of dreaming, and, since we might well be nearing their home territory, I would be reluctant to expose anyone to the danger that this may offer. Belinda and Anthony; are you ready for a long flight?"

The two jumped up, their eyes sparkling, "Yes, yes" said Belinda, and Anthony gave a little skip. Vincent went on, "Off you will go then, but not until tomorrow morning! You need a good night's sleep and a hearty breakfast; it might take you six hours to reach Woodhampton. I will talk to you before you set off, and tell you what you must ask Her Majesty."

Chapter Thirty-one

Brother Adrian took the newcomers to the abbey guesthouse, where they were shown into single or double rooms, plain but comfortable, each with, as well as the bed, a wash-stand, bowl and jug, and a chest for clothing. Kit and Anthony asked to share, and Musgrave invited Belinda in with her, since she could see that the little girl was rather nervous.

All the rooms were lit by candles, with rushlights in sconces in the passageways. Brother Adrian pointed out that a monk was on duty in the guesthouse lobby, saying that no-one should hesitate to ask him if they were in need of any service, and telling them, "Our brothers are dedicated to the comfort of travellers, and this place presents no exception. You will hear the church bell at various times during the night, calling the monks to prayer, but, of course, you have no obligations there. The breakfast bell is different — it is rung along the corridors by a brother; you will recognize it, I am sure. Sleep well!"

Stephen certainly had no difficulty following Adrian's injunction, even though the bed was narrow and firm, and he did not stir until he heard the brother with the handbell passing his room. When he had washed his face and made his way back along the gallery to the refectory, he found his ship's company talking animatedly as they ate their porridge and kedgeree, washed down with goats' milk from the monastery farm.

Vincent and Musgrave took Belinda and Anthony aside, and told them, somewhat to their disappointment, that they would not be flying to Woodhampton that day. Vincent explained that Terence, again a little muddled, had on the previous evening recalled Queen Tabitha saying, when she brought the knights, that she would return to the abbey shortly, so it had been decided that talks with her Majesty could await her arrival.

Neither Terence nor Adrian was present, but another elderly monk offered to answer any further questions, and also, rather eagerly, proposed a guided tour of the abbey farm, "The tide is out, and for the next two or three hours we can walk over the sands to the mainland; I can show you our fields, granaries and stables. I am the one who oversees them, so I would be able to satisfy any of your queries, I'm sure. I am brother Edwin."

Several stood up ready to join the tour, including, of course, Kit, Belinda and Anthony. Stephen demurred, thanking Edwin for the offer, but explaining that he needed to go back on board the Harwich Venturer and plan various matters with Mr Hobson and Sir Maximilian. Then Vincent asked whether he and Musgrave would be able to talk with Terence later in the morning. Edwin explained that the abbot was accustomed to spend the time between Lauds, at about 8 o'clock, and midday community prayers in quiet contemplation, reading and prayer, but that in these exceptional circumstances he would have no hesitation in breaking with this routine, "I will go and talk with him." said Edwin, "Those coming to the farm with me, please wait a few moments; I will not be gone long, and then we can set out."

As Edwin had predicted, Abbot Terence cheerfully ushered Vincent and Musgrave into his office. "I apologize if this feels a little chilly," he said, "for obvious reasons we cannot have fireplaces in our abbey. If you wish, you may tuck a rug round your knees. Now, what can I help you with?"

Musgrave opened the conversation, "Sir Abbot, you have, I'm sure, a general idea of the purpose of our quest, which is to find who or what is responsible for the campaign of assault and terror to which our townspeople have been subjected. And, having identified their source, to take such measures as we can to procure an end to these nuisances. We have arrived here on our way to Grimsby, thinking that, since there appear to be Nordic connections, it might be a suitable place at which to start. Perhaps you can suggest somebody reliable who we may talk to first?"

"Well, thank you for your opinion of me," replied Terence, "but I must admit that, as a member of an enclosed order, I have no real knowledge of other than the spiritual needs of our local inhabitants. But we have, within our ranks, a more worldly soul in whom I have a great deal of confidence. I speak of Samuel Halvorsen, who is our trusted bailiff.

It is he who deals with the sale of our crops and the milling of our grain, and he is responsible for buying our supplies, so he has personal knowledge of many merchants and of the burghers of the town. I believe he is planning to visit Grimsby town today, while the tide is still low. Perhaps one or two of you would like to accompany him?"

Both Musgrave and Vincent eagerly agreed to this suggestion; the abbot rang a bell, and soon brother Adrian appeared.

"Dear Adrian, do you know whether Mr Halvorsen has yet left the Abbey? I would like to know whether he would agree to be accompanied on his trip today."

Adrian left, and was soon back with a large red-faced man with an impressive moustache and whiskers. Vincent and Musgrave had decided between them that Kit would be the best emissary on this occasion. It would appear natural that the bailiff might have an assistant; and until the adversaries were known, discretion was essential.

Halvorsen readily agreed, saying that even if the touring party had already left for the farm, he could overtake them and, at the stables, pick out a suitable mount for Kit.

Less than an hour later, the two were taking the high road to Grimsby.

Chapter Thirty-two

Kit was pleased to find that the riding practice he had on Derek's pony was standing him in good stead; he was able to manage the horse that Mr Halvorsen had picked out for him quite well, although it was much taller than the pony.

As they trotted along, they chatted. Halvorsen asked what Kit hoped to find out in town, and seemed quite satisfied with his explanation, even though Kit was careful not to disclose too much, merely saying that there had been strange events back in Woodhampton that the expedition had set out to understand. Kit got the impression that the bailiff was a practical man, interested mainly in business and trade, and not too bothered with broader issues. However there were a couple of occasions when Halvorsen suddenly looked more intent, causing Kit to feel he might have said too much.

One these followed what Kit thought was an innocent question, "They tell me, Mr Halvorsen, that Grimsby was founded long ago by the Vikings; your name sounds as though you might have connections with those times, is that so?" Halvorsen looked hard at Kit, but then went on freely enough.

"Aye, you're right, young sir. My great grandsire came here from Jutland, but, of course, that was long after the time that the Vikings were raiding and plundering these parts. Once Grimsby was settled, there was a lot of trade between the two countries — there still is, for that matter; you'll often see ships from Copenhagen and Esbjerg in Grimsby harbour these days."

After an hour or so, the two horsemen were approaching the outskirts of Grimsby. Unlike Woodhampton, there was no city wall; the town had no real need for that sort of defence, being surrounded by marshland and approached only by a small number of causeways.

Halvorsen said he had to make a few business visits, and invited Kit to come with him, or, if he chose, to explore the town by himself on foot. Kit chose to keep with the bailiff, and the first call they made was to the windmill that stood near the seaward boundary of the town. The business was to do with setting a price for the coming season's wheat, rye and barley milling for the abbey, and was soon concluded. Halvorsen explained, as they rode away, that the miller was well-disposed toward the monks, and liked to keep on good terms with them, as they were substantial customers for milling.

"You will be interested in the next visit, after what I was saying about Denmark," said Halvorsen, "I have to see a merchant who handles much of the Danish trade here. He, like me, has northern forebears, his name is Magnus Svensen. The monastery buys cheeses here that come from Denmark and Holland (the abbott prefers them to the cheeses we make ourselves), and many other goods that come from further east."

This gave Kit the opportunity to pursue a further question; again it was one which caused Halvorsen to look quizzical, but Kit judged that the risk was worth taking. "So, it sounds to me that there could be many people of Viking or Norse descent in Grimsby; do they form a separate community in among the English-born residents? I have heard from more than one of our company that there are, for instance, inns here which attract people who have common interests in the northern past."

Halvorsen seemed to hedge as he answered, "Of course there are districts where there are more with those connections than there are people who have been English for several generations, but I couldn't say that they amount to close circles, not in the way you are hinting. I myself have friends and business acquaintances of Norse descent, as well as those from old English families."

At that point they arrived at Svensen's warehouse; leaving their horses with a young lad, they made their way up to a loft which looked out over the main storage area; Kit was introduced to the merchant, a tall blond man with a slight limp, who ushered them into his office and waved them to a settle. Halvorsen said that Kit was a visitor to the abbey who had expressed an interest in his work, and the merchant seemed to accept this.

The two businessmen soon launched into talk of goods, prices and delivery times, and Kit listened to the discussion for a while without particular interest until the bailiff and the merchant switched from English to another tongue, Danish he assumed; with his gift, he had no difficulty following the conversation, but he tried to conceal this, mainly by peering around the lower floor at all the activity there. Thus misled, the two discussed some matters of intense interest to Kit, making it even more difficult to affect an air of incomprehension; however he felt that that danger had passed.

Halvorsen opened this private discussion thus, in the Danish language: "*Magnus, my friend, now is the time for great care. These interfering folk from Woodhampton are getting closer and closer to some secrets of ours.*" Svensen looked alarmed at this, "*What have they found out — do they know about Queen Tabitha's sister?*" "*No, not yet, I think. They are expecting the Queen in the next day or two, so it may behove us to make some diversion before she arrives, otherwise she may well decide that now is the time to explain matters more fully to the Woodhampton people. So far, she has been exceedingly circumspect.*"

Kit felt his heart fluttering; here was information that he had to share with Vincent and the others without delay. He waited for a slight break in the conversation, and then addressed Halvorsen, "*Mr. Halvorsen, if I may be so rude as to ask; have you nearly finished your business?*" Then he realised, with a sickening wrench in his stomach, that he had mistakenly spoken in Danish!

Chapter Thirty-three

For what seemed an eternity, but was probably only a matter of seconds, Kit felt as though his heart had stopped. And then Halvorsen answered, in English, "It is I who must apologize for boring you, young sir; Mr Svensen and I have indeed concluded our business, and we shall leave very soon. I have one more call, and then we can set off back to the abbey."

Kit saw to his great relief that neither of the two had even noticed that he had spoken in Danish; their faces betrayed no sense of alarm, which they would certainly have done had they thought he had overheard their secrets.

Svensen accompanied the two out of the warehouse, pausing to point out to Halvorsen a consignment of flagons of wine in plaited straw baskets, saying "I'll warrant that your abbot will be pleased to see some of this fine Rhenish wine; it is a fair time, I think, since your stocks were replenished last."

The horses were left in the charge of the young warehouseman, Halvorsen explaining that his next call was within easy walking distance. Their destination was soon revealed as an imposing town-house, surrounded by a high wall with an iron gate. The bailiff pulled on a bell-rope; quickly a manservant appeared, who, greeting Halvorsen by name and style, led them up the front path. Inside the double oaken doors of the house, he asked them to take their ease on chairs in the entrance hall, while he went to inform his employer.

Kit looked around the hall, which was sumptuously provided with elegant furniture, tapestry wall hangings and oil paintings in gilded frames. One of the paintings which caught his eye was a formal family group under blossom-laden apple trees, showing what looked like a nobleman and his wife and their children, with a pair of greyhounds with jewelled collars sprawled out on the turf at their feet. The two daughters, of about eighteen and fourteen years, seemed faintly familiar to him, and then he realised why — they bore a strong resemblance to Queen Tabitha; in fact the younger of the two may well have been the Queen herself.

While he was puzzling, the manservant who had welcomed them appeared and invited them through more double doors into a large reception room, even more richly decorated than the hall. At the far side, seated on what might almost have been called thrones, was a nobly-dressed couple who appeared to be in their late middle age. The man spoke first, "Good morrow, Halvorsen; what business are you offering me today, and who have you brought to see us? For his benefit, I should introduce myself and my wife. I am Lord Morgan of Louth and Lincoln and this is my wife, Lady Letitia. Could we have your name, my young friend?"

The bailiff bowed, introduced Kit simply as a visitor to the abbey, and went on to explain that his concern today was the renegotiation of a lease that had been granted by the monastic order to his lordship over certain monastery lands. Lady Letitia rose, and approaching Kit, took his elbow, saying, "If I know aught, this bargaining will take for ever and sound particularly dry; let us leave them to it, and you can tell me more about yourself." With that, she led Kit into a small sitting-room, placing him next to her on a long settee, and ringing for a maid whom she sent to bring refreshments. Kit was intrigued to hear that her voice had a trace of the same accent as that of Queen Tabitha.

"Now, Christopher, or may I call you Kit? Mr Halvorsen says you are a visitor to the abbey, but that does not tell me why or how you come to be there. Please indulge an elderly woman with little to occupy her and tell me a better story than that, if you please. Perhaps I should break the ice and tell you what I have found out already about you and your companions; should I do that, Kit?"

Kit had a feeling that Lady Letitia was playing with him a little, but decided to humour her, since it might lead to useful disclosures on her part. He looked her in the eyes, saying, "Please do, my lady, and I will try to fill in any missing parts, if I can. So, if it please you, tell me all you know about our enterprise."

He saw on her face the slightly puzzled expression he had seen once before, when he asked the owner of the Mary Elizabeth for his price, so he was hardly more astonished than the lady herself when she started by listing all the members of the party, from Vincent and Lady Musgrave to the humblest deck-hand from the Harwich Venturer. But, as he marvelled inwardly at this, she went on, giving a big sigh, which Kit felt expressed her relief at unburdening herself of a secret she may have been carrying for some time, "I am kin to Her Majesty Queen Tabitha; she is my cousin, and so also, of course, is her older sister, Lady Margarethe. Those two had a falling-out years ago; even I do not know the true circumstances of it, but it left them estranged, and I'm sorry to say, in the case of Margarethe, considerably bitter."

"I believe that the strange manifestations that you and the people of Woodhampton have been enduring represent an attempt by Lady Margarethe to wreak revenge on her sister Tabitha. It is all very sad. I believe that Tabitha has been at pains not to divulge any of this sorry tale to anyone outside her immediate family, in the hope it could all be handled discreetly, but it has got out of control. Some of those who Margarethe enlisted as her helpers have seen the chance to make profit out of it. I would warn you that it is likely that bailiff Halvorsen may be one of that band. Please be very cautious with him, I entreat you! I am happy to say that I am fairly certain that my husband is not involved in this plot, but since he has dealings with Halvorsen, I have chosen not to confide in him yet."

"Now what I know about your company, apart from all their names, is that several of them are adept in the old arts; Vincent, and Beatrice Musgrave particularly, I also know that you, Belinda and Anthony can change your shapes at will," — Kit forebore to correct her at this point — "and that the others, including Captain Stephen, have no magical powers but are all valiant and masters of their respective callings.

I have also heard that you, Kit, can commune with the Queen's great dogs. And you will already have found out that Queen Tabitha has the power of dreaming, as does her sister Margarethe — to my sorrow, I, although their kin, have no such powers, except that I can from time to time direct my own dreams. Now tell me whether I have this properly."

Kit, although obliged to speak truthfully, did not feel the necessity to fill in all the gaps in Lady Letitia's account, but merely confirmed all that she had mentioned, and admitted that he had lost the power to change shape. His gifts of tongues and veracity could stay private for the present.

Chapter Thirty-four

Lady Letitia seemed about to respond, when there was a tap at the door and the maid came in with a tray of small cakes and pitchers of drinks.

"Are you peckish, Kit?" Letitia asked, "It must be a while since you took your breakfast, and in my experience, young lads and lasses of your age have appetites like wolves!"

Kit helped himself to a cake and a beaker of cider; Lady Letitia took only a cake, which she then crumbled without eating it.

"Now," she said, "let us talk more about your quest. I have no wish for you to divulge anything secret, but, as we have seen, I already know much about the history of these strange affairs. Have Vincent and Beatrice made plans for your further enquiries?"

"Not as far as I know," replied Kit, "and they will, I'm sure, be very interested in what I tell them when I return to the abbey. I will of course acquaint them with what you have told me, and with the facts that I have overheard earlier today. Begging your pardon, my lady, I would prefer not to recount those to you before seeing Vincent and Lady Musgrave."

"You need not apologize or explain, young sir, I would think less of you were you a blabbermouth! Let me put some of my own thoughts to you, and than you can gather all these parts together when you rejoin your company."

"First of all, I have said that Lady Margarethe appears to be the instigator of these events, and that she has drawn together a ragtag and bobtail band to help her carry them out. As is ever the case, this recruitment has opened her up to the danger that some of those who have joined her might be reprobates who would seek to turn things to their own advantage; as it is said: who lies down with dogs risks rising up with fleas!"

"I have said already that I mistrust Samuel Halvorsen; beside dealing with my husband (who I believe to be honorable and honest — but I may well be biased!), he also has business with many in Grimsby. As you have no doubt found out, there is a strong likelihood of a connection in this sad business with those who descend from the old vikings. Halvorsen certainly has such a family connection, and there may be others he deals with who are in similar positions. We in this city conduct much trade with Denmark, Norway and other countries who have natural affinities with the old norsemen. I myself come from Danish and Netherlandish stock, as do my cousins, the Queen and Lady Margarethe, and we all have family back there."

Just then, Lord Morgan and Halvorsen appeared at the door, Morgan saying, "I'm sorry to break up your tête-à-tête, but Mr Halvorsen must head back to the abbey now, so Master Kit should take horse with him. If you wish to continue your conversation later, I'm sure we can arrange something. Were you not saying, my dear, that you must visit the abbey when your cousin, the Queen, pays her next visit shortly?"

Letitia confirmed this with a nod and a smile, then asked Halvorsen and Kit whether they would "Take a sip of sack for the ride home?" Kit politely declined, and so did Halvorsen, but Kit had the feeling that the bailiff was reluctant to refuse, or perhaps had something on his mind, as he was regarding Kit with a somewhat baleful eye, and appeared to be eager to speak to him, but was biting his tongue.

They were shown out of the front gate of the mansion, and headed down the street towards Svensen's warehouse. As they neared the yard where they had left their horses, Halvorsen could restrain himself no longer, "Now, you jackanapes, I suppose you think you hoodwinked me and Magnus over knowing the Danish tongue! Well, you did for a while, and I don't think that Svensen has noticed yet, but something his lordship said to me a few minutes ago made me realize that you had said 'forretning', the Danish word for 'business'. So you must have understood everything we discussed, and know that we intend some action — well you will all find out soon enough, but we can't have you telling the Beeman and his witch about it before we are ready!"

This outburst had taken them up to their horses, who were then led out onto the street by the lad who had been minding them. Kit grasped the pommel of his saddle, put his foot in the stirrup, and was about to mount, when Halvorsen caught hold of his leg roughly to pull him down. But before he could do that, there was a rush and a growl, and a great black dog leapt on his back and bore him to the ground. The second of the Queen's hounds circled the two, with his hackles raised, ready to give help, and then barked out a warning to Kit, which he understood to be "Ride swiftly, young master — you must get to the sea-house as soon as you can!"

Chapter Thirty-five

Kit, startled, took a moment to react, but then, with hands and heels, he urged his mount into motion.

Looking back, he saw that the black dogs had allowed Halvorsen to get to his feet, but also that the bailiff's steed was following his own, leaving Halvorsen abandoned, gesticulating angrily and shouting. Kit was glad he was too far away to be heard, for he guessed that the language he was using, whether English or Danish, would not have been complimentary.

The horses were apparently both used to the journey, for they took the high road seaward without needing further direction from Kit, and soon settled into their stride. And then Kit heard his horse remark to his companion "It will serve the man right, I hope he has to walk all the way home!", while the other one whinnied his agreement. Apparently these intelligent beasts had Halvorsen's measure. Kit, however, feared that the bailiff would soon borrow a replacement from Svensen or another associate, so encouraged his horse to increase his pace. In less than an hour, they entered the gates of the abbey farm and drew up at the stables.

Two lay brothers took charge of the horses, as brother Edwin came out and greeted Kit.

"Why, where is Mr Halvorsen?" he asked, "I hope nothing bad has happened to him. Although I like him not, I would not wish him harm."

Kit answered truthfully, as he was constrained to do, "He is still in Grimsby. I came on ahead without him; I expect he will arrive later. Now, have I missed the tide? Will I get to the island with dry feet?"

Edwin chuckled, "Have no fear, young sir, your captain and his longboat will come for you as soon as I signal." With that, he went over to a flagstaff next to the stables and hoisted a green flag.

Thanking him, Kit walked down to the jetty that jutted out into what was now the bay; earlier in the day, when he and Halvorsen had walked across from the island, it had been high

108

and dry, but now the tide was in. No sooner had he reached its seaward end than he saw the longboat approaching, with Anthony proudly beaming all over his face as he sat at the tiller, next to Stephen, who was apparently teaching him to steer.

As the boat drew close to the jetty, one of the rowers held out his oar for Kit to catch hold of, and the craft was soon close enough for him to step aboard and take a seat in front of Anthony. Then the longboat was pushed off, and they were soon heading for the island.

Kit was eager to relate his adventures, but he held back, not wanting to have to tell the same tale many times, merely congratulating Anthony on his fine helmsmanship, and thanking Stephen for coming to pick him up.

"Why, Kit," said the captain, "you were needed back with us as soon as maybe; Her Majesty Queen Tabitha has arrived and we are looking forward to sharing with her all that we know. I guess you will have some news for us, too; she told us what her dogs reported to her of the behaviour of Halvorsen, and we are agog to know what that was all about — all the dogs could do was tell what they saw and did."

Once at the island, Stephen took Kit and Anthony directly to the locutory, where the others were engaged in general conversation. As they entered, Queen Tabitha rose to her feet and beckoned Kit to approach her; she embraced him warmly and said, "Now Kit, we have all been wondering what befell you in Grimsby — my dogs have told me that they prevented a bad man from hurting you — we have gathered that the man in question must have been Halvorsen. Now, Kit, please start at the beginning and tell us all your story."

He started by telling about the call at the mill, giving as his opinion that the miller was merely a business contact and not part of any plot. Svensen, of course, was another matter; he was clearly implicated, as was Halvorsen, as his remarks about "the Queen's sister" had shown. And then Kit related all that he could remember of what Lady Letitia had told him; his audience was very attentive to this. Finally he described the final altercation with Halvorsen, and thanked the Queen for sending her dogs to rescue him.

"Why, my dear young friend, I did but send them as a precaution, as I commonly do. It is to their credit alone that they took such timely and effective action."

Chapter Thirty-six

When Kit finished his account, there were one or two questions on detail, which he handled confidently.

Then Vincent rose to his feet, "With your permission, Your Majesty, let me set out what I see are the important lessons we have learnt this day. The first, and most important, is that we are on the right track. We embarked on this quest assuming that there was some human agency behind the mysteries that were plaguing us; we find that this seems indeed to be the case — Lady Margarethe, and the minions she has gathered around her, are clearly those responsible."

"Then we thought that there was a distinct Norse flavour to these affairs; now we find that Lady Margarethe's ancestors are from the North, and that at least two of the conspirators also have similar connections."

"Thirdly, we guessed that we could find out more about these happenings if we visited places where the inhabitants and their traditions had connections with the North, perhaps with the descendants of the vikings; and we find that, indeed, Grimsby, a town founded by those Danish invaders, shows evidence of the sort of connections we are seeking."

"Finally, we find, from Lady Letitia and our Queen herself, that what lies behind these events could well be a bitter dispute between family members. If it please you, Your Majesty, perhaps you could confirm this to be the case. Of course, we have no right to know the precise circumstances, and I would not be so impertinent as to ask you."

"Be not so deferential," responded the Queen, "I am not such a fragile flower as to be disturbed by the plain truth! Indeed, the history is that my sister fancied herself offended by me some years ago, and has not grown out of this feeling. It is an old and familiar story, I'm afraid; the elder sister (she is four years my senior) expected from her youth to be entitled to be the first to marry. To her discomfiture, it was I instead who was courted, by Prince Arnold, later our King; and married him, leaving Margarethe unwed and seething over it. She has been fretting ever since, and it has soured her life."

"We must move on," continued Queen Tabitha, "Vincent has reminded us all of the point we have reached in our endeavours; what we do next is going to be vital to our success or our failure. To my way of thinking, there are two roads we can take — first we can treat this as war, and strive to conquer our opponents. I have no doubt that we have the strength and wisdom to prevail in that, though it may take some time. But the second road that is open to us appeals to me more, as a woman (I will hear Lady Beatrice Musgrave's views with interest), and that is the way of reconciliation. It seems to me that such an approach, although it may be delicate and perplexing, might lead to a much more satisfactory conclusion, causing all involved less harm."

Then Musgrave spoke, the tone of her voice seeming to mingle joy and doubt. "Thank you, Your Majesty — I am vastly encouraged to hear your words, as I also am averse to unnecessary conflict. But, I must admit, I am at a loss to know how we can approach these people, some of whom I judge to be out-and-out villains, without risking them taking advantage of us the while. If we were on a field of battle, I venture we could raise a white flag as a sign we are ready to parley, but we are not as plainly situated."

Then up spoke Stephen, "I have never been in a battle at sea, for which I thank God, but I have heard tales from those who have had that experience. Where, in a land battle, the white flag of truce is borne toward the enemy by a single man, clearly not bearing arms, at sea a small dinghy is rowed forward to indicate in like manner that no hostility is meant. Surely we can find ways of telling our adversaries that we wish to discuss terms in a peaceable way. Maybe Mr Halvorsen, though he has been set into a bad mood, might be recruited as an agent for this — providing his temper has recovered when next we see him — if indeed we ever do see him. What say you, Kit? You are the one among us who has most dealings with him, albeit recently in unpromising circumstances."

Kit nodded, but then stopped short, "We are forgetting our dear friend the Abbot," he exclaimed, "if anyone knows how to talk to the bailiff, it must be Terence. And he, as far as I know, has not given him cause to take offence as recently as I have. When Mr Halvorsen returns to the abbey — if he does — I think I should keep out of his way, do you not agree?"

"Yes, indeed!" said Vincent, "But now let us go and speak to the Abbot; I believe that the reason he is not with us already is that he was giving instruction to a group of new postulant monks. Since it is now past the hour for evening prayers, they will be well engaged, and he will be free."

Kit, Vincent, Stephen and Musgrave went to Terence's quarters, to find that he was indeed able to receive them. After Kit had related the occurrences in Grimsby, they asked whether the Abbot was willing to raise the subject with Halvorsen, to which he freely agreed, although, in his mild and retiring manner, he said he was doubtful of his success, "But, at least, I have been dealing with him these past seven or eight years, so we should by now have some common ground. Would any of you wish to be present when I talk to him?"

Vincent demurred at this and so it was arranged that Terence would speak alone to Halvorsen, to find out whether he was open to further discussion, and if he were, then he would be joined by the Queen, Stephen, Vincent and Musgrave, and they would all meet with him together.

But first, of course, they would all have to await his return to the Abbey. Terence dispatched faithful brother Adrian to find out whether anyone on the island or on the farm knew of the bailiff's progress. But he had hardly left when they all heard a commotion in the lobby outside the Abbot's quarters, and then Halvorsen burst into the room, red-faced and furious, Adrian clinging to his arm in a mild attempt to restrain him.

Chapter Thirty-seven

In the confusion, Kit took the opportunity to slip out of the room unobserved by Halvorsen, who had approached the Abbot angrily, while not seeming about to make any physical attack on him or the others.

"Did you know that this ... brisling ... was a spy when you asked me to take him to Grimsby? He has been spreading evil tales about me to some of my most respected business associates. And, to cap it all, he steals my horse, so I must beg my friend to lend me a mount so I might return here. I want this wretch punished, or I will have to do it myself!"

"Now, now, Samuel," replied Terence. "calm thyself, please do. The lad meant no harm, I'm sure. Did you not lay hands on him angrily? He probably took fright at that, as many another would do in the same circumstances; you are a large powerful man. What tales did he spread, and to whom?"

The bailiff did, indeed, seem to pull himself together. He asked if he might sit, and collapsed onto a chair, mopping his brow and breathing less harshly. Musgrave took the opportunity to address him.

"Mr Halvorsen; we have heard from the Abbot that you have been a faithful servant of the abbey these past several years, and we have no reason to believe otherwise. What, then, was it that Kit said that has made you so indignant? And to who was it divulged?"

"Well, your ladyship, I must confess that I may be jumping to conclusions. Just before we left Lord Morgan's mansion, your young friend was deep in conversation with Lady Letitia, and as we left she looked at me very strangely; but now I come to think of it, she has treated me coolly on previous visits, before your party ever arrived in these parts."

Vincent, having heard all of Kit's account, wondered whether Halvorsen's main concern was what might have been overheard of his discussion with Svensen, and that his reactions were therefore born of a guilty conscience, but decided to say nothing yet, especially that the bailiff had apparently thought better of building the events up into a major issue.

Then Halvorsen turned to brother Adrian, saying, "I'm sorry if I brushed thee away before, I did not wish to offend thee; could you now do me further service, if Father Terence will permit it. I believe that one of the businessmen from Grimsby, Mr Svensen, may soon arrive at the abbey farm with some of his men.

If you would kindly see him on his arrival, and give him the note I shall write, I would be very grateful. Sir Abbot, may I borrow paper and a pen?"

He sat a small side desk, and wrote a few lines with a quill. Then he blotted the note with another sheet of paper, folded and sealed it and handed it to Adrian. "Please make sure he reads this before he does anything else, brother Adrian. Now, lady and gentlemen, I must return to my office; the work will not do itself. My apologies to everyone over this commotion."

He left the room, ushering Adrian ahead of him, and closed the door.

As soon as he was gone, Vincent strode to the desk and picked up the blotting-paper. He took it to the window and held it so he could see its reflection; by now it was getting dark outside. "Yes," he exclaimed, "I can make most of it out, though some words were already dry before he blotted the paper. Here we are — *'Magnus, my friend. Something ... ... abandon our plan for the moment ... ... when I see you next. Pay off your men and swear them to secrecy. We will take it up again ... . Samuel.'* "

"Well, this confirms some of our guesses, does it not. This discovery may well affect how we step next."

Chapter Thirty-eight

Vincent turned to Stephen, "Now, Captain, let us follow Brother Adrian; if Kit is still to be found outside, we will take him with us; I want to see this Svensen and his men, and observe how they receive Halvorsen's missive."

As they left Terence's office, they indeed found Kit, who told them that he had waited out of sight for Halvorsen to leave, not wanting to miss whatever was going to happen next. The three set off briskly along the gallery, and it was not long before they heard Adrian up ahead, shuffling along in his sandals.

"How will we reach the farm?" asked Kit, "I supposed that the longboat crew had returned to their quarters."

"We shall use the abbey punt," said Stephen, "as the brothers always do. There are always a pair of them on call in case the punt is needed."

And, as they emerged from the refectory building, Stephen led them to the place, on the opposite side of the island from the Venturer's moorings, where, indeed, two brothers were already helping Adrian down into the punt, an ugly-looking craft with a flat bottom. They joined Adrian, and the other brothers untied the punt, and, grasping a long quant each, started to pole the clumsy vessel toward the far shore. Stephen pointed out that it was guided by a chain, which was laid on the sea-bed and passed through loops at each end of the craft.

While they progressed, Vincent explained to Adrian that he should wait for Svensen alone, while Vincent, Stephen and Kit stayed out of sight, but in a place where they could watch and overhear what transpired. Adrian was obviously a little puzzled, but, being accustomed to follow orders without question, raised no objection.

The three took up their position inside the stable building, where they had a good view of the farm gates; Adrian sat himself on a hay-bale outside and took out from his sleeve a book of the gospels or some such devotional text, in which he was soon immersed, while Stephen, Vincent and Kit occupied themselves in much speculative talk about what their opponents, especially Svensen and his cohort, might be planning.

116

They waited for over an hour, and started to wonder what was taking Svensen and his men so long, but just as they were beginning to think they would never arrive, they heard horse's hooves and the rumble of wagon wheels and spied a group of perhaps seven or eight horsemen and two more on a farm cart, which appeared to be carrying a number of barrels and some bales of straw.

Adrian rose to his feet and called out, "Is Mr Svensen among you, gentlemen, I have a message for him from Mr Halvorsen."

Kit recognized Svensen, on one of the leading horses. He swung himself down and took the paper brusquely, unfolded it and read it. Then he addressed his men, "Well, boys, it looks as though our friend Samuel has lost his courage. Now he wants us to go back to town with our tails between our legs. Well I, for one, do not agree with him; what say you? do we proceed with our plan or do we waste all our effort?"

There were shouts of agreement from the troop, "Aye, let's go ahead and burn the stables down! — Come on, mates, where's the tar and the straw? — Set to, we'll soon have a fine blaze going!"

And Svensen seized poor Adrian by the shoulders, telling one of his burly assistants, "Tie this one up, we don't want him giving the alarm! And have a look round and see if there are any more of these holy friars that we need to shut up, as well!"

Chapter Thirty-Nine

While two of the ruffian crew cast about to see whether they could find any more monks, the others started to unload tar-barrels and straw from the wagon and pile them against the front wall of the stables. Seeing this, Svensen bellowed at them, "Not outside, you dolts, make a big stack in the middle between the horse-stalls, under the hay-loft."

He led the way into the stables, swinging aside the main doors, which were not locked; but was immediately confronted by Vincent, Stephen and Kit, standing shoulder to shoulder just inside. When he saw them, Svensen burst into mocking laughter, crying out to his men, "Look who we have here to stop us! One old gentleman, one man who looks as though he might have some fight in him, and a little boy! Are you afeared, lads?"

A general murmur and some jeering signified that they were not.

Vincent did not reply, but simply raised both hands, palms forward, and stood completely still in this pose. For several seconds, Svensen just looked at him, and then started to laugh again.

But then they all heard a humming sound, at first faint and seemingly from all directions. It soon became louder and then everyone could see its source — a huge swarm of bees, so thick that it blacked out the faint evening light.

And then the bees were attacking Svensen and every one of his men, while sparing Vincent and his companions. In no time each of the would-be assailants was wearing a thick coat of bees, and then they were all screaming in agony as they were stung repeatedly.

At a word from Vincent, Kit ran and untied brother Adrian, who had been roughly shoved on the ground outside the building. The bees paid no attention to him, nor to the two monks who had poled the punt and now ran up with Edwin, the stable-master. Edwin hoisted a signal flag, red this time, saying, "There is one in the refectory building whose duty it is to look out for my signals. Red means 'help' and, as soon as the punt reaches the island, there will be many on their way to give us whatever assistance we need. But," he added, with a chuckle, "it seems that we shall not need any more than a few hands to lock these poor souls away in one of our store-rooms."

Adrian was sent back to the island with the two punt-men, with instructions to ask Abbot Terence to make sure that Halvorsen was kept in his quarters and guarded by a couple of stout monks.

"We shall have a number of questions to ask Halvorsen — and Svensen, too, as soon as he can speak again." said Vincent, with a grim smile.

Later that evening, there was another conference in the locutory. The Queen congratulated Vincent, Stephen and Kit, saying, "We are fortunate that the impulsive — nay, rash — behaviour of Magnus Svensen, and, to a lesser degree, of Samuel Halvorsen, far from advantaging our opponents, has delivered us useful information and the opportunity to obtain even more. Had they not shown their hand in such a way, we might have taken much longer to reach our present position, do you not agree?"

"Yes, your Majesty," replied Musgrave, "I have sometimes thought that we have been too circumspect in our enquiries, but now we are striding ahead confidently. If I may make a suggestion, now could be the right time to make a direct approach to Lady Margarethe, since we have something more than conjecture to base it upon. I take it, ma'am, that you have ways of communicating with her, apart from dreaming; would you be willing to open a conversation with her, after all these years of reticence on both your parts?"

"I can do better than that, I believe," said the Queen, "I am ready to invite her to a neutral place where we can speak face to face. I would guess that she would not be averse to meeting us here in Grimsby, at the house of the lady Letitia, our cousin. Master Kit, would you be willing to raise the idea with her ladyship?"

Chapter Forty

Kit readily agreed to be the emissary to Lady Letitia — he had rather enjoyed their last conversation and had been sorry to have had it cut short.

So plans were laid for the next day; Vincent insisted that, before Kit should leave for town, Svensen must be catechized searchingly while he was being held at a disadvantage. If he would talk at all he might let slip some item that would be valuable in bargaining. Said Vincent, "I shall be excessively kind to him; I will offer him my secret salve that will soothe his stings very swiftly — I can warrant that it works, from personal experience! He may not be the sort that is easily grateful, but after a night in a cold store-room with every inch of his skin burning he might well open up to me!"

There was also some talk about who might be a suitable companion for Kit on his mission. After some discussion the decision was made that Stephen should go as protector — there might still be some of Svensen's knavish crew lurking in wait for Kit — and Lady Beatrice Musgrave would ride with them, to add her persuasive skills to the task of asking Lady Letitia to help set the scene for what might very easily become disquieting exchanges between Queen Tabitha and her sister.

They all went to bed with their heads full of the coming events; nevertheless Kit was asleep as soon as his head met the pillow. The next morning, Kit joined Stephen at breakfast, to be told that Vincent and Musgrave were already at the stables with Svensen and the other rueful members of his now comic troupe. But, by the time that the two had eaten and drunk their fill of wholesome Abbey fare, Vincent and Musgrave arrived, in somewhat of a jubilant state.

In answer to Kit's eager questions, Vincent disclosed that, not only had Svensen talked freely about his failed exploit of the day before, but had also made it clear that, now his blood had cooled, his misgivings about the whole enterprise were rising to the surface. He now claimed that Halvorsen had forced his hand, holding the threat of lost business over his head. He had also offered the opinion that Lady Margarethe had been having second thoughts about the course of her campaign; Svensen had

120

only spoken with her once, a month or so ago, but on that occasion she had seemed sad and apprehensive that the whole matter was getting to be more than she had intended.

So it was in a cheerful mood that Kit, Stephen and Musgrave set off from the farm on their way to Grimsby town, Musgrave riding pillion to Stephen, and this feeling still persisted as they drew up outside the gates of Lord Morgan's manor house. The watchman at the gate recognized Kit, greeting him cheerfully, and went to see whether Lady Letitia would receive them. He soon returned, and they were ushered straight into the modest sitting-room where Kit had chatted with her ladyship only the day before.

After only a few minutes, Lady Letitia joined them, and was introduced to Musgrave and Stephen by Kit. She greeted each of them warmly, kissing Musgrave on both cheeks in the Netherlandish way, and shaking Kit's and Stephen's hands.

"Well, it is a pleasure to have such visitors," she said, "I do like Grimsby in the main, but there is no society here — I sometimes take carriage to York merely to have converse with lady-friends, drink their wine and beat them at cards! That is where cousin Margarethe lives, but I cannot say that I move in her circle very much; however, many of her friends are at least known to me. I am guessing that your visit here must be somehow to do with your quest, so might involve Margarethe in some way; am I right, or is this one of my wishful phantasies?"

Kit replied, taking his mission seriously. "Well, my lady, you are certainly right. We may be being presumptuous, but we are here to ask you if you would act as a go-between, and even a hostess, for Queen Tabitha and Lady Margarethe, hoping that a reconciliation might not be completely out of the question."

"Oh, I am so glad to hear you say that! I will eagerly do whatever I am able — as I told you last time, Master Kit, I regard the estrangement between Her Majesty and Lady Margarethe as a very unfortunate and sad affair; it would be a wondrous thing if it could be brought to an end to the satisfaction of all."

Then Musgrave joined in, saying, "I expected nothing less from you, Letitia, if I may address you thus, since Kit told us of the opinion you expressed to him. I, too, am filled with hope that we may be able to achieve such a rapprochement. But it is, of course,

121

very sensitive territory and we should tiptoe into it, rather than emulate the blundering efforts of Magnus Svensen. By the way, I should relate these to you, together with the way that our resourceful Vincent dealt with them only yesterday."

At this point, Lady Letitia, always hospitable, rang a bell for the maid, suggesting that they should proceed with their planning over a light repast. And then they settled down comfortably to await that and to hear Musgrave's account, which she presented in high dramatic style.

Chapter Forty-one

When they had all listened with some interest and amusement to Musgrave's tale, which she enlivened with imitated voices and actions, and after they had eaten of their fill (or picked at their food, depending on their ages and appetites), Musgrave asked Lady Letitia if she might turn to a more apposite and intriguing topic, to which suggestion she received her hostess' immediate assent, as well as that of the rest of the group.

"I should like," said Musgrave, "to acquaint those of you who are open to new experiences (as you all are, I believe) with a few of the marvels and strange and valuable outcomes that can be brought about by dreaming. You have heard how Queen Tabitha has the gift of travelling with its aid, and how she can transport others, such as our brave knights, even though they do not possess any of these so-called magical powers themselves. In this group today there are myself and Kit, who have both shown that we have certain magical gifts, and Stephen and Lady Letitia, who have no knowledge of whether they have them or not. Let me conduct an experiment in natural history for you."

"Please sit comfortably, as you would at at the end of the day, contentedly, with your bellies full, your bodies loose and your minds calm. Now, close your eyes and pay close attention to what you will hear from me."

Stephen, with the others, obeyed her directions, as she began a low tuneless humming, and he had no difficulty in directing his thoughts only to that. After a few minutes, he could discern what might have been the beginnings of speech, but was not able to distinguish the words, nor even the language she was using, and found his mind turning to a scrutiny of his surroundings. And then, he realized he was asleep and knew he was dreaming. He opened his eyes and looked about.

They seemed still to be in Letitia's small sitting-room, but he felt he was floating near the ceiling; indeed he could see himself sitting, eyes closed, on his chair, and the others likewise on theirs — even Musgrave, whose voice he could still faintly hear. And then, as he watched, a fifth figure appeared, seated on a wide settle, gradually taking the form of Queen Tabitha. He hung marvelling at this for a while, and then closed his sleeping eyes as Musgrave's song changed and became louder and more insistent.

And then, all of a sudden, he woke up fully, back on his chair, and looking around saw the others rousing themselves; including the Queen, who now stood and addressed them all.

"My dear people," she said, "I must thank Lady Beatrice Musgrave for this little play. Of course, we put our heads together this morning, back at the abbey, so that I would be ready to dream myself here. What think you all of this?"

Kit was the first to speak, "Every year while I have been Vincent's assistant, friend or prentice, he has shown me new miracles (if that is not too much to call them). When I was but a chubby-cheeked youngster of five or six years, he showed me that I could change my shape, and then over the next years carefully instructed me in the proper ways of using that gift, so that it might always used for good and not for idle play. And when, as I knew it must, that gift left me, Vincent gave me new powers, less exciting, perhaps, but more profoundly useful. Now, I realize that there are many more adventures left for me, should wise Vincent deem me worthy of them. Thank you, Vincent, and Your Majesty, and Lady Musgrave for today's revelation. I begin to see that we are well-equipped to resolve our quest."

Stephen had a question. "I marvel at what has now been divulged to us; these abilities certainly have much to offer us as we seek the solution to what started as a complete mystery and has now shown itself to be a conspiracy, albeit one of an elevated nature. But I am a practical man at heart, so I must ask some practical questions: how we are to proceed, and what exactly are we to do next?"

Then Lady Letitia spoke up, too, "The Captain is a practical man, and I am but a woman of some frivolity, but I too have wondered about our next moves; I have offered this house as a stage upon which we shall play out our drama. When will the curtain rise, and what is to be the first scene?"

Musgrave rose, saying, "By your leave, your Majesty, I promise I will answer these questions; but I prefer not to do so in the absence of our other companions, not only Vincent, who of course is central to our work, but also the other members of the Woodhampton party, and our allies at the abbey. We should all gather here again tomorrow, if Letitia will agree, when we can properly plan our campaign."

"Of course," said Letitia, "I will cause my large reception room to be made ready. Shall we forgather at noon tomorrow?"

Chapter Forty-two

At the appointed time the following day, a substantial procession arrived at Lord Morgan's mansion. First came the Abbot's coach, with Terence, Vincent, Musgrave and Queen Tabitha inside, and Anthony and Belinda riding up front with the abbey driver, a lay brother called Badger (Stephen recalled that the King's coachman was called Weasel, and wondered whether this sort of naming was traditional for coachmen). Then there were the horsemen; Kit, Stephen, Mr Hobson, mate of the Venturer, Sir Maximillian, two of the knights from the bluebell wood and Brother Edwin, the abbey stablemaster.

The coach and hackneys having been taken round to the mews at the back of the house, the party was conducted into the main reception room, and greeted by Lady Letitia and by Lord Morgan, who explained that he had been put in the picture by his wife, was merely there as an observer, but would be ready to assist in any way he could. After the necessary introductions of all members of the party, Letitia brought forward a young woman of studious mien, saying. "This is my niece, Abigail, who often acts as my amanuensis; she will keep a record of any evidence that we think vital and any decisions we make. Please let her know if there is anything you would specially like her to note."

Vincent thanked Letitia for her hospitality and opened the discussion.

"We all agree, do we not, that it will be essential to negotiate directly with the lady Margarethe, once we are sure that she is truly the originator of all the assaults we have seen — we cannot, of course, hold her responsible for the recent ridiculous acts of Halvorsen and Svensen. Paradoxically, that rash adventure may prove to be a key to opening our dialogue; what if we start by announcing to her that we do not hold her at all at blame for the attempted arson of the abbey stables? Will this not give her the chance to express regret at some of the other manifestations that she might be wishing had never taken the course that they did?"

"I am with you, Vincent," said the Queen, "but what I am still uncertain about is how we should approach Margarethe — I mean, who would be the best person to do it, and in what way?

126

Maybe, Letitia, if you are willing, she would regard you as a sufficiently disinterested emissary? How do you feel about this?"

"I am completely happy to act thus," was the reply, "I can even make a suggestion as to the way it could be done. As I told Kit the other day, I frequently travel to York, where Lady Margarethe lives, and I could call on her there. She is bound by common courtesy to receive me, and I can carefully broach the subject once I am presented with a suitable opportunity. As it is customary for a person of my station to be accompanied by a lady-in-waiting, perhaps dear Beatrice would not mind acting in that role; I would certainly feel more confident were she with me."

Musgrave agreed, adding, "And it would be prudent if Her Majesty the Queen, Vincent and others could be waiting close at hand while we make our advances and entreaties to Lady Margarethe, so that we may seize whatever opportunities may arise. And, in passing, this prompts me to think that we should arrange some way of passing messages from us inside the house to those in waiting outside; I shall ponder on this."

There followed general discussion, and finally the composition of the delegation was agreed. As well as Letitia, Musgrave, Tabitha and Vincent, it was decided to send Stephen, because of his long involvement and his experience of loss, Kit, with his gifts of tongues and veracity, and Belinda, because of her own special powers. The consensus was that the party should not be larger than that; the last impression that should be given Lady Margarethe was that they were in any sense an army.

"And, of course," said Vincent, "we must be prepared for Margarethe not to receive us, or worse, not to be in residence. Tabitha reassured them all on the latter point, saying that she had thought of this and paid a dream visit not an hour since, and that Margarethe had been in her house, and that no preparations for an imminent journey had been evident.

Late the next morning, a coach drew up at a fine mansion in one of the fashionable streets near the centre of York; a liveried servant helped an elegantly-dressed lady carrying a fluffy white lap-dog out of the coach, while another rang at the street door and spoke with its custodian. With little delay, a butler emerged, bowed to the lady and invited her inside, together with her female companion, a tall grey-haired person of obvious dignity.

Vincent (the first servant) and Stephen (the second) rejoined Tabitha in the coach, while the coachman and Kit took their ease on the box to maintain a steady lookout. The street was soon teeming with ladies and gentlemen, strolling in couples and greeting their acquaintances, while smart drinking-houses in the adjacent side-streets began to do a brisk trade.

Chapter Forty-three

The butler showed Letitia and Musgrave into the mansion. Inside the front doors there was a small lobby, which then gave onto a spacious hall, decorated, somewhat like Letitia's, with tapestries and large oil paintings. Musgrave noticed with interest that one of these appeared to be by the same hand, and painted at about the same time, as the family portrait in Letitia's house; this depicted the same noble couple and the same two young women, but this time the greyhounds were not shown; instead the father held the bridle of a fine white stallion.

As they were ushered onward, Lady Margarethe advanced to meet them, taking Letitia's hands and acknowledging Musgrave with a nod that was amiable enough, but bearing a slightly puzzled expression on her powdered and heavily-rouged face.

Letitia immediately took the initiative, "Thank you so much for receiving us," she said, as Margarethe led them to a sitting room and beckoned them to be seated. "You will no doubt be somewhat puzzled to know the reason for our visit, which is patently not simply a social call."

"You are right," responded Margarethe, "perhaps you could tell me! Will you take refreshments the while?" and she called a footman over and gave him instructions.

"I will not waste time any further; you may recognize me as your cousin, although we have not met for some years. I am Letitia, wife of Lord Morgan of Louth and Lincoln, and this is my friend Lady Beatrice de Gonville Musgrave. I live in Grimsby, as mayhap you know, and Beatrice is from Woodhampton, where is the court of King Arnold and Queen Tabitha. Perhaps this begins to give you a hint of our purpose in visiting you, which I can assure you is conducted in a friendly and open spirit. I go further — the Queen is desirous of achieving a reconciliation with you, my Lady."

Letitia rose and drew nearer to Margarethe, touching her arm gently, "Have you knowledge of the recent activities of one Magnus Svensen, who is, I think an associate of yours?"

Margarethe sprang to her feet and raised her hands in a gesture of alarm; "Speak not of this Svensen! I dearly wish that I had never met him, nor his ally Samuel Halvorsen. Why I ever thought ..."

She sat once more and dabbed tears from her eyes with a kerchief. "What has he done now — nothing good, I would hazard!"

"As it so happens, it was no more than an attempt, swiftly thwarted by our dear friend Vincent the Beeman and his swarm, to burn down the stables at the abbey of Louth Minor, near Grimsby. A heinous act indeed, but one that we are all convinced could never have been countenanced by you, my lady. From the way you have just reacted, it is easy to see that you never intended to cause real harm to anyone, from Woodhampton or elsewhere.

"Oh, you are right, you are right; I had the foolish notion of frightening my sister Tabitha, in spitefulness for the slight I felt she did me years ago. But it all got out of hand ... You say that she is eager for reconciliation; I welcome this whole-heartedly and long to beg her forgiveness, face to face. I hope that it can be soon."

Letitia, smiling, embraced her and then beckoned the footman, handed him her little lapdog, and murmured some instructions to him. He straightway took the dog to the front door and went out with it.

By this time, Margarethe was sobbing, but Letitia, patting her, said soothingly, "Now now, my dear, wait a few moments and you will have your wish."

Meranwhile, in the street outside, the little dog ran up to the coach and was lifted into it by Kit. Once inside, Belinda resumed her own shape and prepared to relate all that had transpired to Tabitha and the others.

Chapter Forty-four

After Belinda had told all that had happened, the Queen descended from the carriage, took Vincent's arm, and followed by the rest of the group, approached the doors of the mansion, where the footman was still waiting. She spoke briefly to him, and he opened the doors, and preceded them, announcing as he entered the hall, "Her Majesty, Queen Tabitha and party."

Margarethe, who had been standing with Musgrave, holding her hand, hesitated a few moments, and than darted forward and flung her arms around her sister, who hugged her in return; both women were by then weeping freely. Musgrave led them into the sitting room and closed the doors, saying, "Let us give them time to become reacquainted; they have not conversed as sisters for many years."

She, Letitia, and the others made themselves comfortable in the hall, and the footman brought them drinks and small cakes. They chatted of inconsequential matters for at least half an hour, until Tabitha and Margarethe appeared, hand in hand, still somewhat tearful, but both with shy smiles. Margarethe spoke.

"We have agreed that I owe it to all of you to present my history of the disturbing events of the past few weeks; I am grateful to have this opportunity. I will not make excuses, for my actions are inexcusable, but I hope that you will all have some sense of peace when I have finished. Please come back into the sitting-room and settle yourselves down while I tell my tale."

Margarethe sat on a small upright chair, facing her guests, who were on low chairs and settles along one wall. She started by taking them all back two or three months, to the first strange incidents at Woodhampton — food turned into stone, animals behaving strangely, vanishing babies, people who had lost the power of speech. She explained that each of these was to a degree as unexpected to her as it was strange to the victims; "I do not know how to do any of those things; I am not a witch or a sorceress — what I did was to accept the aid of someone with such powers, in a misguided sense of trust. If I had realized soon enough and if I had the strength of will, I would have called a halt there and then. But now, I am not sure I would have been

131

heeded, for by that time my accomplice had the bit between her teeth and would have been difficult to rein in."

"I suppose that, for you present, the incidents of most interest would be, first, the great wave that struck Captain Stephen's ship, and second, the extraordinary business in the bluebell wood. Let me tell you first about the wave; as we all have discovered since, the ship was undamaged and not a precious life was lost. But I was mortified to hear that everyone, including Stephen, was convinced otherwise — and who would be surprised at that — so I wrote anonymously to Vincent, telling him of Stephen's distress. I was not yet ready to confess my involvement in all this plotting — I must have still been completely bemused; at the time, I truly did not know that the creation of such a wave was possible, but once I heard that it had happened, I was appalled, and that is why I made sure that a message about it reached Woodhampton Castle."

"So Vincent and Lady Musgrave decided that Kit should be sent to find Stephen and distract him from his grief by recruiting him to the quest to find the source of all the enchantments; what foolishness, that I should have stood aside and allowed this charade to continue!"

Margarethe paused at this point, and moistened her mouth with water. Her audience could see that the recounting was difficult for her, but at the same time was providing her with some relief.

Tabitha took the opportunity to ask a question that she had been fretting over during Margarethe's story.

"But what perplexes me," she said, "is why you ever embarked on this ill-considered, dare I say it, altogether foolish enterprise. I remember, from our childhood together, that you were ever a mite impulsive, but to go to these lengths, merely in a fit of pique ..."

Margarethe clasped her hands together and wrung them agitatedly. "It was our old nurse, Griselda, who encouraged me — nay, dragooned me — into this. You must recall that I was ever her favourite; she had me to her own for four or five years, but when you arrived, Mother fancied she would take an interest in us both — we were a charming pair to parade before her friends — and Griselda was pushed into the background. She resented you from that time onward, and lately, as her faculties

132

dim and her mind begins to stray, she fancies that she can once more be my guide and protector — but it was not Griselda who conjured up all the happenings, as I will explain in a little while."

Chapter Forty-five

Stephen was about to ask a further question, as he was anxious to find out how Margarethe knew of the wave and of his distress, but he held his tongue for the moment, trusting that more would be revealed in good time. Margarethe was obviously committed to making a clean breast of it all. As he had hoped, Lady Margarethe drew herself up and continued her story.

"As well as inciting me to take revenge on my sister, for slights that she had resented, it appears, much more than I, Griselda introduced me to her relative — a niece, I believe — who she claimed was possessed of puissant magical and occult skills. I must admit that I was repelled by this young woman at first sight; but again, sadly, I had not the strength of will to repudiate the assistance she offered at that time. She was called Ulfrigga — a Norse name, I am told — she was spare of figure, almost haggard, with matted hair, and spoke only in harsh whispers."

"To convince me of her powers, this ... creature called me to the window and pointed to two doves flying; she made a gesture and muttered some words, at which the two innocent creatures plummeted to the earth. She spoke another phrase and I could see them rouse themselves and start to walk about. This gave me an idea — for which I have been thankful ever since — and I enjoined her that, whatever she did on my behalf, she should ensure that no permanent harm would come to man nor beast. She agreed, though she was obviously puzzled why I thought it necessary, and Griselda assured me that she was bound by the laws of her esoteric craft to keep to this promise."

"Ulfrigga was still insistent on demonstrating her powers. From inside her ragged garments she drew a small hand-mirror, such as ladies use when they wish to see whether their faces are presentable in company. She handed it to me and bade me look into it earnestly. I took it from her and did what she wished, but I could discern nothing in it but swirling clouds, like the mist which rises when the sun first strikes a meadow in the morning. Ulfrigga then made some gestures and uttered some words that I understood not. As I looked into the glass, it cleared, and I beheld a stretch of open sea, upon which a ship sailed. And then, as I watched in fascination, I saw a great wave arise and dash against the ship, completely swamping it. I called out in alarm and distress, but the weird woman grasped my arm and bade me wait. And then I saw that the wave had abated, and the ship had recovered."

As her audience stirred and looked at each other in amazement, Margarethe proceeded with her narration.

"If anyone wishes to question me further, let them, please, indulge me for the moment and wait a little. That demonstration by Ulfrigga, as you will understand, was the beginning of a series of conjurations that she performed. I constantly prevailed on her to cause no lasting harm, and she as constantly reassured me that she would not. She kept charge of the hand-glass, but from time to time used it to show me the outcomes of her magicks. When she showed me that a young man, whom I later found to be Captain Stephen, had survived the effects of the great wave, was unharmed but was trudging wearily towards Woodhampton, I decided to let my sister and her court know of this, so that he might be relieved of his fatigue and distress. I visited the castle in a dream, but found that Tabitha was not in residence, so I conveyed the message to Vincent instead. You know what happened after that."

There was much murmured conversation following this account. Margarethe refreshed herself with a draught of wine, and answered the deluge of questions that followed. Stephen first took the opportunity to thank her for her compassion for him; then Musgrave asked about the attack in the bluebell wood, and, in particular, about the so-called river of rats, saying that she could understand that the stupefying vapour was one of Ulfrigga's tricks, but that the rats were different in some way.

Margarethe explained that Ulfrigga had seen the toy rat in the old nurse's quarters — it had been sewn by a lady of the household as an exercise in embroidery and as a present for the girls, long before, and had simply taken delight in showing how she could multiply it many times and set them all in motion. She added "And as for the grave-pools and the message in runes left on the road, my dear sister can tell you more than I. If you will all excuse me now, I am afraid that this unburdening has left me feeling weak, as well as greatly relieved."

Chapter Forty-six

Lady Margarethe all but staggered to a comfortable chair and sank into it, dabbing at her face with her kerchief. Vincent conferred briefly with Musgrave, who then went over to Margrethe and, with the help of a maid, led her out of the sitting room and up to her bed-chamber. Returning, Musgrave addressed the group.

"I have nothing but admiration for the brave way that Lady Margarethe has disclosed her story; it must have been very trying, even shaming, for her. But now, in return for her sincerity and bravery, we must see in what ways we can help her. From what she has told us, nurse Griselda and the witch Ulfrigga will not be easy to dismiss, and we know that others have been drawn into the plot, like Halvorsen and Svensen."

Vincent was quick to endorse this statement, "Indeed, dear Beatrice, we must now steer our efforts in a new direction; but I feel mightily encouraged, since we are now entering an open contest, instead of fumbling in the dark. What, your Majesty, do you say on this; are you willing to carry on being involved yourself, or would you prefer to leave the struggle to us?"

Queen Tabitha responded vigourously, "I know your suggestion is not heartfelt, but merely a matter of courtesy, Vincent, so I am not offended by it. However, at this stage, I can assure everyone present that I could no more bring myself to withdraw from this enterprise than to take up something ladylike, such as tapestry or the playing of the spinet! But, as dear Beatrice has pointed out, we may have difficulties with Griselda, and, I must admit the possibility that any confrontation with Ulfrigga might be perilous indeed; in this modern age the power of witches has come under threat, and she could draw on all her dark arts in a frantic attempt to resist us."

Kit had a question: "Will the gifts that Vincent has bestowed on me be effective on such a creature as this Ulfrigga? Will she, like mortals, be obliged to tell me the truth when I desire it? I know not what powers these witches can draw upon in their ungodly work. And if she can resist my modest gifts, would she be powerful enough to combat those of Vincent and Musgrave? Lady Margarethe seems to have fallen under her thrall, but is

Ulfrigga simply taking advantage of her uncertain determination and weakness of will?"

Vincent reassured him, saying that a righteous power will always prevail against one used for evil, and added what was needed from the company was help for Margarethe to strengthen her resolve, as well as ways of dissuading Griselda and Ulfrigga from pursuing their misguided campaign, a notion that raised a further question for him.

"Does anyone know where Griselda and Ulfrigga can be found?" he asked, to which the Queen replied, "We shall have to ask Margarethe; the last I saw of Griselda she was still in residence here, but I seem to recall that she was willed a cottage by our father — he died seven or eight years ago — on the family's country estate, a few miles north of York. As for Ulfrigga, the first I heard of her was today; I have no knowledge of where she can be found. Let us wait until Margarethe has rested, and then, no doubt, we shall find out more.

At that moment, the butler entered, and with discreet cough, addressed the Queen. "Your Majesty, would you and your companions care to come with me to the dining-room, where a light luncheon has been prepared for you? Lady Margarethe instructed the staff to prepare such a meal earlier today, before you all arrived, and I am sure she would not wish you to wait for her."

All were happy to comply with this suggestion and were shown through the reception room into a fine dining-room, with a long table arrayed with choice dishes of cold cuts, cheeses, breads, fruits and wine. As they eagerly fell to, Stephen drew Vincent aside, saying, "If I know aught of the ways of great households, I would guess that the butler would know everything that goes on here; should we not ask him if he could tell us of the whereabouts of Griselda and Ulfrigga?" "A capital suggestion," replied Vincent, "we can always rely on you, Captain, to sort out the practical from the conjectural!" and he beckoned to the butler and engaged him in a quiet dialogue. After a few minutes, he slapped the butler on the shoulder happily and turned back to the others.

"Good news!" he exclaimed, "We shall not have to wait long to confront the dastardly duo! As soon as Lady Margarethe is herself again we can see them, for they are both, at this very moment, in the upper rooms of this house!"

Chapter Forty-seven

It was late afternoon before Lady Margarethe reappeared. She had washed her face and changed her clothes and appeared refreshed and relaxed.

"If you have all had your fill of food and drink," she said, "perhaps you would like to join me in the sitting-room once more; I'm sure you wish to discuss what is the best way to proceed, what we should do next, is that not so?"

There was a general murmur of assent, and the company proceeded to move back to the sitting-room and settle down in a group, having dragged the chairs and settees into a circle. Vincent was the first to speak.

"My lady, please excuse us for taking liberties, but we have found out from your staff that Griselda and Ulfrigga are likely in residence, here in your house; which offers the opportunity for us to confront them immediately, if you consider that would be wise. It seems to me — I would like others to give their opinions also — that we should not delay long, and yet we should not act too precipitately. We must assume that they are aware of our presence here, and have guessed our purpose; it would be foolish to underestimate them. But if we move too suddenly they may take this as a sign of aggression."

Both Margarethe and Musgrave seemed ready to respond to this; Musgrave realized this, and withdrew with a gracious gesture, signalling the other to speak.

"I understand what you are saying," Margarethe said, "and I agree with your arguments. But I do not believe we should treat both Griselda and Ulfrigga in the same way, or, indeed, at the same time. I have had many dealings with both of them, and, although I may have been behaving in a naive way for too long, I have some grasp of their several characters. Remember that my old nurse was the one who instigated this black play — and I do not shy away from my complicity in it — and that Ulfrigga was recruited by her. So my suggestion is that we should first tackle Griselda. It may well be that, once we have convinced her to abandon her efforts against Queen Tabitha and all her supporters, we shall have little difficulty with her familiar, Ulfrigga."

Musgrave stood and clapped her hands. "Bravo," she exclaimed, "I must congratulate you, my lady, and say how gratified I feel that you have found the strength to confront Griselda, after so long being intimidated by her — please forgive me for these bold and impertinent words, Margarethe."

Queen Tabitha, Vincent and Stephen briefly spoke to add to these sentiments; Kit and Belinda simply smiled and nodded.

Margarethe rang a bell, and soon the butler appeared at the door. She addressed him:

"Mr Partridge, please go and bring Nurse Griselda here. Just Griselda, no one else; you will know who I mean. If she appears angry or reluctant, you have my permission to explain to her in whatever way you think fit, that we simply wish to discuss matters with her, and not to accuse her of ill-doing. Don't hurry her — allow her whatever time she needs to prepare herself."

While they waited, Stephen was concerned about the arrangement of the furniture.

"Should we not try to avoid the appearance of a trial?" he asked, "If we seat her — or make her stand, even worse — so that she feels she is in the dock, confronted by her accusers, this will make it likely that her behaviour will be defensive, will it not?"

So it was decided that she should take her place as one of the circle; across from Vincent, who would be the main speaker, and with Queen Tabitha off at one side. Kit suggested that he be positioned so that he could speak directly to her, should it be thought apt for him to bring his gift of veracity into play.

They had all settled to their assigned places when the butler knocked at the door and entered, bringing with him a tiny bent figure, dressed all in widow's black. "Nurse Griselda Kraneveldt." he announced; and Musgrave took her hand and led her to her seat.

Chapter Forty-eight

The nurse sat peering around her, obviously confused, so Margarethe went round the group, naming each of them in turn, with a brief explanation of who they were. Griselda simply nodded as the names were said, but her expression remained one of puzzlement.

Then Letitia rose and approached her, taking her limp hand and saying, "Nurse Griselda, I am Lady Letitia de Morgan, a cousin to Lady Margarethe and to Queen Tabitha; we have met a long time ago, but you may not remember me. As you probably understand, I have no direct interest in this affair. I am with neither side in this dispute or misunderstanding, and have no right nor reason to judge your actions, whether favourably or not. So, if you will permit me, I will begin asking you some questions; you may answer or not, as you wish."

The nurse looked bewildered, saying in a small wavering voice, "Yes, my lady; but I do not understand what misunderstanding it is that you talk of, and I do not know who are all these people. I see Miss Margarethe, and you tell me that other one is little Miss Tabitha, but they have grown up very much. Why are you all here?"

Letitia glanced at Vincent and the others for reassurance, and then spoke gently to the old woman.

"If you do not know, my dear, we will bother you no more. Master Kit, would you ask Griselda if she truly knows not why she is here, if you please."

Kit paused by Vincent, who spoke a few words softly to him, and then went and knelt on one knee in front of the nurse, looking into her eyes.

"I am a friend of Margarethe and Tabitha. Please tell me, nurse, do these sisters have a quarrel with one another?" The nurse shook her head, again looking bewildered. "And do you know aught of any spells or like magic that have been cast against Tabitha?" Again, the nurse shook her head, saying "What is this foolishness, what have I to do with magic?"

Kit asked a final question "Do you know what business Ulfrigga, your kinswoman, has with Margarethe and Tabitha?"

Again the nurse shook her head, and began to weep, "I don't understand, I don't understand!" she cried, and then Musgrave went to her, comforted her and gently led her out of the room.

As soon as she was gone, an excited hubbub of talk burst out. Vincent raised his hand for silence and said what many were thinking, "The poor soul has lost her wits and can remember nothing of recent times. I have seen this before with very old people; she could probably give us a day by day account of her upbringing of her two little girls, decades since, but as for yesterday or last week, it all disappears into the mist."

"So, we had better speak to Ulfrigga, then," said Tabitha, "Margarethe — do you wish to be here from the beginning of that, or do you think it better to excuse yourself for the nonce? I would agree with either course, it is your decision."

Margarethe thought for a moment and then replied that she would like to be present, but not to take any part in questioning Ulfrigga until it became clear how she intended to respond.

"So," said Vincent, "unless anyone has any further comments, shall we fetch Ulfrigga? When Beatrice returns, if she is willing, she might be the best one to go and find her, with the butler to guide her and with Stephen to stand with her in case Ulfrigga should lose her temper."

And so, when Musgrave came back into the room, reporting that she had seen the nurse into the care of a maidservant, who was to put her to bed with some warm milk, she agreed with the plan, and, the butler having been called, left with him and Stephen.

More than an hour elapsed, and there was general fidgeting in the room, as people began to wonder about the delay and advance guesses about the reason for it. Then the three emissaries came back, evidently alarmed. Musgrave exclaimed, in a somewhat dramatic way, "She has vanished — Ulfrigga has escaped us — we made enquiries among the staff, and one little girl says she saw her, wrapped in a cloak, leaving on foot through the vegetable garden not two hours ago!"

142

Chapter Forty-nine

This announcement caused general consternation, of course, but Vincent, always a steadying influence, appealed for calm.

"Let us keep our heads. Your Majesty, Ladies and Gentlemen; we should carefully consider our next moves — we need to find and talk to Ulfrigga, it is true, but nothing is to be gained by rushing off in all directions at once!"

"Lady Margarethe, with your permission, I would like to ask Mr Partridge to bring us this little kitchen-maid, or whoever the child is, so that she can point out in which direction she saw Ulfrigga leaving. And, Your Majesty, I would also be so bold as to suggest that we have a ready-made task here for your black dogs, if they have aught of the bloodhound in their make-up."

The butler left the room immediately on his quest, and Tabitha stood up, "I thank you, Vincent, if I had more forethought I might have had my dogs here already; I think you are right — they are the ones to help us. Please settle down, everyone, and I will go into the next room and dream a little. Meanwhile, Captain Stephen, since you now know where Ulfrigga's quarters are, perhaps you could go there and bring down some article of hers, clothing or bed-linen, that my dogs could sniff for a scent to follow."

The queen left, and shortly thereafter the butler returned, bringing with him a little girl of about seven years, barefoot and wearing a soaking-wet apron over her long dress. "This is our youngest helper, Polly," he announced, "don't be fearful, child, no one here will scold you or harm you. Take that apron off, do, or you will catch your death."

"I was in the middle of a-scraping of the carrots, Sir," she said, with a certain spirit, but did as he said.

Vincent beckoned her to him and told her why she was wanted. She seemed pleased by the attention, and eagerly started her account. "I seen that old Ulfrigga out the winder, when I was fetching some wood for the stove, she was walking right through the cabbages — Mr 'Obbs the gardener would a been riled — to a gap there is in the kitchen-garden wall, where we allus goes through to the woods to pick blackberries, but when they're in season, not now. I could show you, there's a regular path when you gets through." She gave a little squeak then, as she saw Tabitha bringing her two black dogs into the room. Vincent patted her on the head and made her sit down against the wall to wait, as he thought that she was too grimy for the brocade chairs.

Tabitha made an announcement, "I need not introduce my good dogs to Master Kit, but for the others of you who may not have met them, here are Joris and Hero. You can tell them apart, because Hero is the one with the scar on his shoulder. This is the legacy of a joust he had with a boar two years since, when the beast essayed to unhorse me as I rode along the slopes up above Woodhampton Castle."

The dogs nuzzled Kit's hands as he fondled them, then Joris turned his attention to Belinda, as she stood rather hesitant, not knowing whether to pat them too, and put his muzzle in her hands. The Queen smiled, saying "He can recognize that you were but recently a little white lap-dog, Belinda. He will do no more than sniff you, though!"

Vincent asked her, "Your Majesty; I have assumed, as I said, that these fine creatures will be able to track Ulfrigga by scent — is that indeed so? Have you employed them thus?"

"Not to track a person, Vincent, I have had no occasion to do so; but they have no difficulty with deer or foxes or even badgers! One feeble witch-woman will be no problem, I'm sure, unless she realizes she is being dogged and lays a false trail, or worse, puts down some potion that will harm my dogs. Let us hope she will not guess this. But, enough talk of tracking, let us set to and do it — here is Captain Stephen with some clothing for the dogs to sniff."

Before very long, Stephen, Tabitha (who insisted on going, despite protests from Letitia and Musgrave), Kit, and Vincent were following the dogs along a path through the woods, having been shown the gap in the garden wall by little Polly. It was soon clear that Joris and Hero had picked up the scent, as they whimpered eagerly and wanted to break into a run; Tabitha had to restrain them by a series of commands in a tongue which Kit could follow, though he knew not what it was — not Danish — while he could also understand the remarks passing back and forth between them.

They soon left the woods and the path led them up a slight slope onto moorland, where they followed the path for what must have been more than a league. Then, cresting a low ridge, they caught sight of a cloaked figure some way ahead, who was apparently tiring or having some difficulty with her legs, as she was becoming slower with every yard. Then she noticed her pursuers, and to their surprise, flung herself down on the turf at the side of the path.

When the party came up with her, the dogs took up positions beyond her, and she painfully pulled herself up to a sitting position, saying, "Well, you have me now, Your Majesty, you must treat me how you will, for I have no more the energy to resist you, and I deserve your wrath."

Chapter Fifty

Filled with compassion, Tabitha knelt by Ulfrigga's side and rested a comforting hand on her shoulder — a dreadful mistake. With a triumphant cackle, the witch threw her cloak over Tabitha's head and clutched it together, trapping her arms. As Vincent and Stephen started to recover from their stunned astonishment and move forward, Ulfrigga sprayed a red powder from her mouth onto them and they were frozen in place. But she had forgotten the dogs and had underestimated Kit.

Joris launched himself at her back, knocking her over; then Hero seized her arm in his jaws and wrenched it aside, so she lost her grip on the cloak and Tabitha was able to roll clear. Meanwhile, Kit, to his own astonishment and that of the others, found himself transformed into an immense serpent, and quickly trapped Ulfrigga in his coils, so her limbs were trapped and her throat constricted. He explained later that he had felt an immediate impulse to strangle her, but that his training, received from Vincent over the years, had made him forbear.

Tabitha regained her feet as Vincent and Stephen shook themselves back into action; the red powder apparently acted for only a short while; they seemed to be none the worse for the enchantment.

After a few moments, the Queen began humming tunelessly, as Musgrave had done when she demonstrated her dreaming powers, and Ulfrigga's eyes fluttered and then closed as she became unconscious.

Kit uncoiled and became a young man again, and helped Stephen and Vincent bind the witch firmly with the cord from her cloak and cover her face with Stephen's kerchief.

"Well!", said Vincent, "that was all very entertaining! Shall we do it again?" The ensuing burst of laughter broke the general bewilderment, and they started to breathe normally once more.

Kit lost no time in enquiring of Vincent how it was that he had been able to transform into a serpent, and was assured that his power had been briefly reawakened by the extreme urgency of the situation, but that he might not ever experience it again.

"Now," said Tabitha, "we have a new problem; what are we to do with this unfortunate soul? We can hardly leave her loose, since there is every chance she will fall back into her foolish and malevolent ways once she is free and conscious. I can transport her to a more secure place; she is yet in the dreamworld and it will be quite simple for me to dream her somewhere where we can decide what to do. Shall I do this, and where?"

Vincent responded promptly, "An excellent notion, Your Majesty; might I suggest that Louth Abbey would be the best destination? We can keep her securely there, and our friends, Abbot Terence and his monks, will surely be well able to deal with any attempts at magic that Ulfrigga might be tempted to essay."

With that, Tabitha closed her eyes, and, in a moment she and the bound witch faded and disappeared. Stephen found that he had become thoroughly accustomed to such happenings, and hardly blinked.

Within two days, they were all back at the Abbey again, where, amongst other things, Terence conducted an exorcism ceremony directed at Ulfrigga, which lasted for several hours and involved much praying, chanting and the burning of incense. As he confided later, he was not sure that it would be effective, but that if Ulfrigga believed in it, that would be sufficient for her to put an end to her mischief-making.

Stephen and his crew, now including Anthony, who expressed his desire to embrace a life as a seafarer (this was approved by Vincent on condition that he would regularly join Stephen's children in their lessons), made ready to sail back to Harwich, taking Lady Letitia along, who, ever open to new experiences, had begged for the chance for "an adventure at sea". Stephen privately hoped that it would not involve any excitement whatsoever and was looking forward to resuming the more hum-drum trade of a merchant venturer.

Two weeks later, everyone, including Lady Letitia and Lord Morgan, Lady Margarethe, the whole expeditionary party, with the lost knights and other restored souls, not forgetting the Abbot as well as the Mother Superior from the sister nunnery and their senior staff, gathered at Woodhampton Castle as the guests of King Arnold and Queen Tabitha for a grand celebratory banquet.

Ulfrigga was not invited.

After the eating, drinking and chattering came the time for speeches. King Arnold, now walking with sticks, was the first to address the throng.

"My first duty", he said, "is to express our devout thanks to God for our lives and safety, and to all those who joined in this endeavour, and brought it to a successful outcome. To Vincent, Beatrice Musgrave, Osric, Kit, Belinda and Anthony, and our respected sage and teacher, Arbutius; I am so fortunate to be surrounded by a houseful of people of such probity, strength and talent. To my gallant knights, to Erik and to my staff, our thanks also. To Abbott Terence and brothers Adrian and Edwin our gratitude for their hospitality and support. To Stephen, whose navigational skills and crew members were offered to us without hesitation, despite the deep sorrow that rode on his shoulders at the beginning, we shall be for ever indebted. And finally, to my beloved wife, your Queen Tabitha, who bore the threat to her safety with fortitude throughout, playing a vital part in combatting the dark forces arrayed against her and us, and to her sister, the lady Margarethe, who, although she might have felt blameworthy at the start, steadfastly insisted that no harm should ever befall anyone, and finally wrested herself away from the conspirators who had taken advantage of her frailty."

After the burst of cheering and applause that followed this speech had died away, the King raised his hand once more and continued.

"And now, my second duty, or rather pleasant opportunity, is to invite anyone who wishes to address us, about any topic whatsoever, but particularly on how they view the future, now these unfortunate events seem to be behind us. Perhaps I could persuade the Lady Margarethe to start us all off."

This lady at first waved her fan dismissively, but then, with a shrug and a moue, stood up and began.

"Your Majesties, ladies, gentlemen and children, first I echo King Arnold and would thank most humbly all those whom he mentioned; but I would like to add one more name, of one who is not here, my sister's and my old nurse, Griselda. It is true that she was the one who set all the problems in train, but I firmly believe that, had she been able to foresee what would happen, she would never have enlisted the aid of the evil Ulfrigga; her actions were intended to be protective of me, and they were simply taken out of her hands. And this leads me to beg an apology of all present; had I been stronger and more resolute, I should have called a halt to the nonsense as soon as it started; *mea culpa, mea maxima culpa.*"

As she sat down, Vincent rose; looking around the company to make sure he was not talking out of turn, he began.

"Of course I speak for everyone here in saying that we hold Lady Margarethe blameless, and hope she will be able to put all this behind her. But, I am equally certain that every one of us will set forth from this day reinvigorated and even cleansed; we have faced demons and they have been vanquished. I myself, with my faithful family and retinue, intend to make certain that our lives henceforth will be lived with a new probity; I hope that I am not deceiving myself."

"Captain Stephen can speak for himself, but I wish him every success in his ventures on sea and land, and happiness for his beautiful family, who are now joined by my grandson Anthony; may the lad grow up to be a successful merchant venturer like Stephen. And Kit, what of Kit?"

This question, perhaps rhetorical, was answered unexpectedly from a new quarter. Lady Letitia stood and called Kit to her, saying, "I have already asked master Kit to join my husband and me in our business and estate; we are aware that he has special talents that will enable him to represent our interests at home and overseas, once he has learnt the proper principles of business, and I am happy to say that he has agreed to this." She hugged Kit, and Lord Morgan shook his hand warmly.

The last word belonged to Lady Beatrice de Gonville-Musgrave,

"I recall, and is seems an eternity ago, that I stood on the stage outside this castle, relating a litany of the strange and threatening occurrences that first caused us to suspect we were all under attack by a strange and powerful force. Some of these events were merely curious, while others were dreadful, but we were powerless and frightened. Nevertheless, we stood together — from the humblest peasant to the King himself — and we prevailed, with God's help. Let us all contemplate our good

149

fortune for a few moments — and then, may the music and dancing commence!"